"Bloom's cleverly written young adult novel, which begins innocently enough, morphs into a surprising and empowering page turner with an oh, so timely message. Perhaps Ionesco would have appreciated this reinterpretation of his *Rhinoceros* to bring this important conversation into middle and high school social studies classrooms."

—Susanne Meyer-Fitzsimmons, author of
Deep Living: Healing Yourself to Heal the Planet

"Blundertown presents an interesting parallel to what happened in Nazi Germany. Sadly, it may be more relevant than ever today with what is going on in this country."

—Rabbi Michele Brand Medwin, author of
A Spiritual Guide to the World of God, Parts I & II

"*Blundertown* hooks young readers and pulls at their dog-loving heartstrings while challenging them to consider their response when faced with discrimination and injustice: Do they wait, blindly follow, or stand up and take action? As an educator, I recommend this book to teachers and students."

—*Angela M. Church, Berkley High School*
Social Studies teacher, Berkley, MI

THE THING
AT THE EDGE
OF BLUNDERTOWN

3/2020

Mazel Tov to Eli !

THE THING AT THE EDGE OF BLUNDERTOWN

A Young Adult Novel

Jane M. Bloom

Full Court Press
Englewood Cliffs, New Jersey

Published in the United States of America
by Full Court Press, 601 Palisade Avenue,
Englewood Cliffs, NJ 07632
fullcourtpress.com

This is a work of fiction, and any resemblance to
actual persons living or dead is purely coincidental.

ISBN 978-1-946989-35-2
Library of Congress Catalog No. 2019905696

Editing and book design by Barry Sheinkopf

Author photo by Jonathan C. Hyman © arthoops55@gmail.com

To Louise and Rayna
whose love for each other inspired this story,
and to all who stand up to hatred

Acknowledgments

It is fitting that this story came to me in a dream. It was in 2013, a time when we'd begun noticing a change of tone—small but disturbing incidents that occurred far away from here, buried in the news. Then 2016 came along and exposed us all. I dusted off my manuscript; it no longer read as a tale of history, but rather as current events.

I am grateful to the many people who contributed to this book. There wasn't a single critique from friend or family that wasn't spot-on, and addressing each one of them made the story better. In particular, I thank my daughter, target-age at the time, who read an initial sketch and gave the green light to proceed, and my brother, David Hunt, for his wise red pen once I'd finished my first, so-called "final" draft.

I thank Sharon Linnéa and Thomas Mattingly for their invaluable workshop, and my fellow writers Susanne, Micki, and Claudia, whose continued encouragement for another chapter kept me on task.

Additionally, I thank my editor, Barry Sheinkopf, whose instincts and expertise are above reproach, and my husband, Steven Bloom, whose patience and support made writing through the wee hours possible. I am forever blessed by my mother, Nancy Hunt, an avid reader and the best person and mother in the world.

Lastly, I thank Temple Sholom, my spiritual home.

PROLOGUE

WHEN I WAS LITTLE, I WAS A VIVID DREAMER. *By the time I was twelve, all of my dreams had come true. Some grownups spend their entire lives trying to make just one dream come true. But beware: Some dreams you would rather remain just that—silly, nocturnal illusions, prickly nightmares that never reach beyond the bounds of sleep. Trust me that, once you get rid of the bad dreams, there's more room for the really wonderful ones.*

I can't promise your dreams will come true, but I can tell you how it works for me. I just close my eyes at night and wait. Iggy and I hold each other, his stuffed lizard nose nestling against my chin. The scene is as dark and vast as a starless sky. Then, suddenly it's there: The Glitter! First, just a handful of bright, colorful specks appear, so tiny that I'm not sure if my eyes are playing tricks: fluorescent purples, greens, and turquoise. But sure enough, they begin to twinkle at me, Hi, Raelyn! Then, huge bursts of glitter-dust bound in from everywhere: neon orange and jade, translucent gold and silver, pinks, blues and light bulb white—the brightest rainbow explosion! It's my own custom-made fireworks, only instead of filling the sky, they seep gently into my tiny universe of dreams. My belly leaps inside as if I'm racing with my brother Jackson, his knuckles clenched to the steering wheel as he whoops with laughter. But here in the sanctity of my room, there is no fear of crashing or spinning out of control.

Once I've seen this magnificent display, I know that all is right with the world. It's my go-ahead to settle into the comforts of deep slumber. And that is when I have my dreams.

I've seen the Glitter since before I can remember. It has always been with me, except for during the Horror many years ago (which is what I now call it). No matter my yearning, my wondrous, mystical Glitter was nowhere to be found. I was as empty as the bottomless pit Jackson used to tease me about.

I recall the exact day that I lost the Glitter. And I recall the very day that it came back to me.

It all had to do with Penelope.

CHAPTER 1

Greetings

THE BUS SCREECHED TO A STOP, and the doors slammed open in front of 12 Hucklepuddy Road. Raelyn Devine was leaning over a fellow student in the last row, studying the graffiti on the back of the seat. Yes! She'd finally found what she was looking for: the answer to her brother's second clue. As annoyed as she was with Jackson, she would play his stupid game—but only because he had promised there'd be a prize at the end. She couldn't imagine what kind of prize it would be under the circumstances, and, she guessed, neither could he.

His second clue went like this:

> *Dear Baby Rae,*
> *Still working to win back your heart*
> *Not easy when we're apart*
> *You're my little Sis*
> *Whom I deeply miss*
> *And I'm just a great, big old FART!*

— 3 —

So here's the next clue of the Game
A "Who Am I" riddle to name:
Who loves MarCUS?
Hint: see back of BUS
(In rhyming stuff, I'm rather lame.)
—Your Big Bro, Jackass Jackson

"E": the answer was "E" for Emily, forever trapped in a lopsided heart on Bus 36: *"Emily loves Marcus."* An arrow had pierced right through them.

"Hey. C'mon," someone grumbled. Impatient murmurs reached her from all sides. She swung her backpack over one shoulder and her frizzy, black hair over the other as she made her way to the front of the bus.

"Don't forget about *you know what*," Angelica called after her. No way would she forget.

Now that she was in middle school, she was old enough to come home to an empty house and not lose her very own house key. She turned it in a practiced way.

"HELLOOOO, MY LADY!" SHE SANG OUT as her bag fell to the floor. A bundle of shiny black-and-tan fur sassed in front of her. She bent down and gave her dog, Penelope, a tremendous hug. She couldn't recall a day in her life when Penelope hadn't been there to greet her at the door. They'd grown up together. At first, they were both rambunctious little puppies. But for every year that Raelyn grew, Penelope grew seven-fold, so that now she was quite a refined old lady.

And she was a generous kisser. "*Eww*, gross." Raelyn wiped her smeared glasses. "I missed you." She grabbed the thick fur around Penelope's neck and rubbed her velvety ears. They were the softest, silkiest texture ever. The best part was that Raelyn didn't come home to an empty house at all. She came home to her best friend. "How was your day, huh?"

My day? To Penelope, this was a most welcome question. *Well, it was rather peculiar, indeed! So very kind of you to ask.* She hoisted herself up, scratching Raelynn's jacket. As she did so, a mild pang shot through her hind legs. *Arthritis—such a nuisance.*

"Whoa! Calm down, girl." Raelynn lowered her gently. She spotted the kitchen towel in the middle of the floor. "Penny," she demanded, feigning a deep, baritone voice, "why did you do that?"

Penelope stared absently in the other direction. *Who, me?*

Raelyn draped the damp towel back over the oven door (who would know) and ran her glasses under the faucet. She was tall and as skinny as her brother had been at her age: all knees and elbows. On the refrigerator under "Jack's Treasure Hunt," she marked an "E" next to the letter "G."

Then she noticed a slip of orange paper under the desk. It, too, had been slobbered over. She sat on the floor and stroked the top of Penelope's head, mauled document in hand. She buried her nose into the warm fur. The sweet, musty smell was Raelyn's favorite in all the world. "What's wrong, My Lady?" Her mother called Penelope mischievous, but Raelyn knew her better than that. Penelope wasn't naughty; she was upset. She plopped her chin on Raelyn's shoulder, where it rested for a few moments. "Hey!" Raelyn lifted it so their noses touched. "Guess what we almost forgot?" She jumped up and approached a ceramic jar on the counter.

"T, R—," she began to spell. At the second letter, Penelope galloped across the glossy floor and skidded to a stop at her feet. She sat with perfect posture, a single controlled lick of the tongue. Black marble eyes followed Raelyn's arm as it swung backward . . .then forward, the hand overhead. . .and then: the release! Penelope sprang off her hind legs and leaped, catching the treat midair. She was a pro, even in her golden years. It was always worth the minor discomfort.

"Good catch! You're ready for Short Stop." Raelyn laughed every time. "W-A-L-K?"

Penelope pranced in a circle and barked, *Of course, my dear— what a silly question!* She reached into a long, elegant stretch, der-rière high in the air. *Always stretch before exercise—particularly when elderly.* Then she sat, prim and proper, as Raelyn dressed her in her favorite accessory, a stunning pink-and-gold necklace.

THEY LEFT, LEASH IN HAND. The special item from Angelica (a green envelope that had passed through an unspoken chain of students) would have to wait.

Most of the trees were bare by then, with carpets of color at their feet. They shuffled through the autumn foliage. As they approached the neighbors' house, Penny's head sprang up. *Oh, lucky day!* She lunged forward. *Allow me to lead, if I may.*

"Penny, heel," said Raelyn.

"Well, hello, Little Neighbor," Kelly Davis called in the exact same way she always did. She was wearing her blue eye shadow and coral lipstick, and she had a bag of groceries in her arms. She broke all of Angelica's fashion rules. "How've you been?"

"Good." Raelyn stopped. Penelope sat dutifully at her side, her tail making broad sweeps as she awaited the good graces of her favorite neighbor.

Ms. Davis beamed her over-the-top, phony smile and pointed a commanding finger at Penelope. "Stay." She hustled into her house. She had a huge behind and hips that formed a shelf on either side, shifting back and forth as she moved. Penelope's eyes remained fixed on the front door. *Patience, patience,* she urged herself, barely able to sit still. As soon as the door opened, she whimpered, and Ms. Davis instantly rewarded her with a snack. *What exquisite flavor! Quite a delicacy today.*

"Say hi to your folks for us."

"I will." Raelyn knew she wouldn't—how silly. They lived right next door.

They reached the bottom of the hill. Raelyn noticed a few geese gliding in the pond. But Penelope was looking across the street. *"Boxer! Hello, Boxer! It's me, Penelope!"* she greeted him, tugging toward her friend. *"How've you been? Anything new, darling? Yoo-hoo, Boxer? Hello, there!"*

Raelyn coaxed firmly. "No, Penny. Next time."

"She says, next time! Toodle-oo," Penelope promised, and stepped in line. (Had she known there'd be no next time, mind you, she would have been more persistent.)

EVENTUALLY, THEY APPROACHED THE SIGN *Welcome to Blundertown Park.* They'd been coming to the park alone since September. Before that, Jackson used to join them. Now he wasn't going to be home for a very long time—maybe even a year—but who needed him anyway? Certainly not the Raelyn–Penny team. She planned to jog around the bases with Penny to prep for softball in the spring. She was lousy at sports, but the bar was low for sixth graders. They would take anybody. Literally. That was why Gil Richmond shouldn't be so braggy.

She peered into the field. It didn't look as if anyone (Gil Richmond) was there, fortunately. He sometimes came with Prince, his handsome German Shepherd. They would exchange "heys" and let their dogs circle and sniff each other. It was a bit awkward. One, dogs sniffing each other's behinds was awkward. Two, being face-to-face with any boy from school *outside* school was awkward. Three, even Angelica thought Gil Richmond was annoying. He was the star of the cross-country team and had already broken a school record—big deal, since sixth-grade sports didn't even count. He got away with things no one else did because his mother was an assistant principal. And they lived in the wealthiest section of town. One block over, and he would attend Luxmore Middle School with its fancy Olympic-sized pool. So long, been good to know you.

And four, it was Gil Richmond, and it would always be awkward for reasons best left unmentioned.

She noticed a smaller sign to the right of the park entrance that she'd never seen before. She approached it, setting herself in a beam of late afternoon sun. It was the size of notebook paper, with bold black letters. At the sight of the words, she stopped short. Instantly, Penelope sat at her heel. An autumn chill whipped out of nowhere, and a swirl of dead leaves rose up and whirl-pooled around them. She read the sign a second time, but seemed unable to comprehend the three words that appeared:

No Dogs Allowed

Those three words would change both their lives forever.

CHAPTER 2

The Sleuthing Begins

WHEN I WAS SIX, I *dreamed I was a detective, creeping around the house with my magnifying glass. Just as I did in real life, I wore my sleuthing hat and searched under the cushions, behind the chairs, and on tip-top shelves. I didn't know exactly what I was looking for, but I finally hit the jackpot in the bathroom: a mysterious puzzle piece under the sink. "Mommy!" I called, running around the house until I tracked her down. I showed it to her. She said, "That's nice, honey."*

I guess if you don't know what you're looking for, you can't know when you've found it.

"WHY?" RAELYN WANTED TO KNOW over dinner. "It makes no sense."

"Well, I don't know." Her mother sprinkled salt on her plate as if it were magic dust. She did this, and many other quirky things, on a daily basis. (She places exactly one ice cube in her drink, rotates her plate clockwise as she eats, and dabs her napkin with every other bite—and that's just dinner). "There must be some good reason. They wouldn't do it unless there was a reason." Her hair was still in a thin pony tail from work.

"Who is '*they*'?" Rae asked.

"They. Town Council? Parks?" Her mother glanced across the table to Raelyn's father, who was taking in snatches of the newspaper. "Vigil?" she called to coax him out of his private world. He shrugged with his mouth full.

"So where do *they* expect you to take your dog? If all the parks are now closed to dogs? That's insane," Rae concluded. Penelope lay a few feet from the table, concentrating on the environs just below her chair. She knew from years of experience that chances of falling food were best beneath the child's seat. Even though Raelyn kept getting bigger, she was still the child and always would be.

Her father turned another page and rubbed his eyes. "Budget cuts," he said. "They had to eliminate some park jobs. Cleaning up dog poop, it's become a burden on taxpayers." He popped his glasses back on, a gold adornment on an otherwise dark face. "I suppose that's what's behind this new law, I don't know." Whenever the subject was local politics, his voice became a dull drone, like a long, passing train beating on the tracks.

"But, Dad, you *do* know. You're a county legislator."

"Well, but this isn't a county issue, really. It's HR. PD."

"English, please, Dad?" She and her mother exchanged

smirks with matching dimples.

"Human Resources. Parks Department. Sorry."

Her mother slapped the table, a light-green flicker in her eyes. "So that's why our taxes have *doubled* practically overnight?"

"Partly, yes," he answered. "It's more complicated than that, of course." As all politics were.

"Well, in that case, the closings couldn't come soon enough," her mother announced, back in the business of her dinner salad.

"No way," Raelyn interjected. "Everyone picks up. Our park is totally clean. No dogs! That's so *unfair*." She wiggled a few secret fingers under the table. Penny picked up the cue and edged toward her for a little petting *(and perhaps a nibble of something)*. "Poor Penelope! *Now* where can she go?"

Her mother gave a short laugh. "Anywhere but the park, sweetheart."

"Our Gloomy Rae of Sunshine," her father teased, then quickly changed topics. "Not at the table, Raelyn." He'd caught the whole underhanded exchange. Penelope retreated slightly but remained on task.

"Speaking of Penny," her mother smiled, a sing-song in her voice, "guess what I found in the living room? Yesterday's newspaper scattered all over the floor." She looked at Penny with playful disapproval. Penny's tail wagged guardedly. "Oh, and she ate the mail. A flyer." The Devine family's mail came through the bronze postal slot in the front door. Each day a wrapped bundle awaited them inside, but that day a separate leaflet had arrived as well. "It was under the desk in the kitchen, of all places."

"She got into the waste basket in the bathroom, too," her father said, amused. "I can't recall the last time she did that."

"I can." Rae reminded them, "It was when Jackson left."

Her mother read the mangled bright-orange paper that Raelyn had seen earlier but hadn't read. "Says, 'Official Notice, Daffy County: Come join. Ollie's Neighborhood Watch Group.' First meeting Saturday, blah, blah, blah. 'Dog issues discussed, refreshments served.' But the time and place are all chewed off." She tossed it aside. "No matter. I'm not interested in any of that politics anyway."

"Maybe she knows," Rae chimed.

"Knows what? Who?"

"Penny. About the park. Maybe she already knew. Maybe she had a feeling."

"Oh, sweetie." Her mother laughed up at the ceiling.

"Only our Raelyn would think of that." Her father beamed.

"But I'm serious." It was dawning on Raelyn just how much they still treated her like a little girl when she wasn't one anymore. Her chest grew tight with simmering anger, like water before coming to a boil. "Well, it's just a stupid sign. I'm taking her anyway. No one's standing there watching."

"No, you will *not*," her mother chided. "That's breaking the law. You don't have to like it, but, unfortunately, it *is* the law."

"Yeah, tell me about that," Raelyn muttered. The silverware on either side stopped clicking.

"Now, now," her father mumbled.

"Exactly." Her mother was turning pink. "Look where *he* is.

You want that, too?"

"No."

"Then stop talking nonsense." Nonsense was the term her mother used for anything that someone else didn't agree with her about. Raelyn brought her plate to the kitchen. As she passed him, her father was back to reading the paper. "Not at the dinner table, Dad." He folded it and slid it aside. She was faced with that familiar, stern look from them both.

There I go again, she thought, that razor-thin line between safety and trouble. Fortunately, her survival instincts kicked in. She chuckled, "Just kidding, Dad, geez." She glided out of the dining room. The air was suddenly much lighter, and lighter still as she hopped the staircase to her bedroom. Jackson would be proud of her developing skills.

That night, Jackson's letters floated before her in the dark: G,G,G. . .E,E. . .E,G,E,G. What would it be? E,G,G? G,E,E? Other letters joined the mix, an alphabet party with newly arriving guests. G,E,E,S,E? G,R,E,E,D? E,D,G,E? G,R,E,E,N? This was silly. With only two of the six clues so far, it was impossible to guess the final answer. More random characters danced before her now: another D, a couple Os, an S, an N. They suddenly rearranged before her eyes: N,O,D,O,G,S.

It was inconceivable. Going to the park with Penelope was like breathing. She had never known a time that they hadn't. She'd been two when Penny joined the family, a tiny abandoned puppy with a gash above her eye and an intense fear of mops. For years, Raelyn had begged her parents to let Penelope sleep in her bedroom at night. Upstairs was off limits, her fluffy bed at the foot of the stairs as keeper of the household. Of course, her parents won, and Penny never had set foot in the bedroom.

Except once (until the Canine Problem took a turn for the worse; but as to those occasions, the parents never knew). She recalled that eventful summer day. For some unknown reason, Penelope had growled at one of her friends. The girls had only been seven at the time, and Chrissy's screams had startled the neighborhood. Raelyn's mother had rushed out to the porch to see the girl petrified—with Penelope five feet away, a tuft of raised fur forming a threatening line down her spine. Raelyn, too, had been completely still, like a cardboard cut-out in short, woolly pigtails.

"Penelope!" Her mother had swept up Chrissy, who immediately began heaving out of control, shut Penny inside, and returned bright pink, her sandy hair limp and disheveled. When the girl's parents arrived, she'd questioned whether they should find Penelope a new home without children. Raelyn, hysterical, had begged her not to. Her father remained silent, the dark gentle giant of the house. Thankfully, Chrissy's parents had reminded them that they'd known Penelope for years and she was a wonderful dog. But more importantly, she was family. You couldn't just send a family member away like that.

Still, once an idea came to her mother, it stuck like super-glue. Part Two of the discussion had hit a crescendo over dinner. Her heels were dug in: Penelope must go. Mr. Devine had remained on the fence. Raelyn knew what that meant, because her mother always won. She had sobbed at full volume, *"No! Penelope!"* hysterics pouring into the living room, and flung her body over Penny's, crying out her name over and over until bedtime, while Jackson stared into the blank TV screen.

Raelyn had awakened well after midnight. The street light had cast a faded glow into her room. And there was Penelope, lying on the floor at the side of her bed, tail wagging: Penelope! Never in her life had she woken to such a miracle! In the morning, Raelyn had raced downstairs and found her curled-up at the bottom of the steps.

Her parents had been awed when she told them. There was something special there, they agreed. There was intuition, wisdom, a cherished love between their daughter and her dog. It was all too much to lose. Penelope had remained with them to this day. She never growled at anyone again, although mother kept a vigilant eye when company came. Such was the unique bond Raelyn and Penny shared.

RAELYN GAVE UP ON JACKSON'S CLUES and concentrated on settling into her magical Glitter world. First, the familiar, creamy darkness oozed into her mind's eye, like warm chocolate pudding swirling around among the shadows. Flecks of color began flickering about, and the first exciting bursts appeared. A smile blossomed as she squeezed Iggy. The show went into spectacular high gear, with explosions of every color imaginable.

But suddenly, the black-and-white sign at the park interrupted it. She flipped onto her opposite side and rearranged the sheets.

Then she switched onto her belly, ruffling up the pillow. But the three ominous words continued blurring in and out of focus. Just as she was finally drifting toward sleep, they morphed into the chewed-up orange flyer.

Then it turned green.

She sat upright in bed. She'd forgotten the note from Angelica! How could she have forgotten such an unforgettable thing as that?

She turned on the light. It was after ten o'clock. She grabbed her backpack and pulled out the wrinkled envelope. It was from a boy, that was all she knew. Who brought envelopes to school? Whoever he was must have planned ahead. She ripped it open and pulled out a piece of note paper. The penmanship was atrocious, definitely a boy's writing. It was short, just three lines, and ran uphill. The note began, *Dear Ray*, misspelling her name. Clearly, this person didn't know much about her. It continued, *Are you taking Pinelloppy to the park tomorrow? From Gil.*

Gil Richmond, of all the boys! A green envelope. . .are you kidding me?

On the other hand, it *was* her first love letter ever. It counted for something. She pictured him, of medium height with brown hair and dark squinty eyes. His face didn't look much different from when he was five, except his cheeks had been chubbier then and he had acne now. She re-read the letter and began formulating how she should respond. She imagined meeting him with Prince tomorrow afternoon. The dogs would sniff each other as they always did, while she and Gil R. would think of how to look and what to say. She'd heard a first date could be a disaster. Or maybe there would be a connection that would cancel out their humiliating secret. Break that ancient curse. How did any of that happen? she wondered.

Instantly, she realized she *couldn't* respond to his love letter: There *was* no park to take their dogs to. *No Dogs Allowed.* How could they meet at the park when Penny and Prince were not even allowed to be there?

So much for the shortest relationship in human history.

CHAPTER 3

BFFs And What They Wore

WHEN I WAS EIGHT, I DREAMED *that Angelica and I were performing a show for Nobody in her backyard, something we occasionally did in real life. We wore her mother's opera make-up and wacky ponytails all over. But her tap shoes were real, and mine were patent leathers with quarters glued to the bottoms. We danced and sang a song written and choreographed entirely by her. As in real life, I just followed her instructions.*

After our curtsies and standing ovations, we found ourselves by a large boulder near the woods. Angelica had become a princess with a fancy dress and a crown of gold. Her hair was glistening red like her mother's. She scooped up a small decorative box from behind the rock. "What's this?" Her blue eyes sparkled like sapphires.

I grabbed it out of her hands. "That's mine! Don't open it."

She was bewildered. "Why can't I see what's inside?"

"Because they're secrets." I hovered over my box and refused to let her touch it.

"Best Friends never keep secrets."

"I know," I tried to explain, "but you can't see them. Please don't be mad."

But she was, and she stormed away without looking back.

"So?" Angelica whispered during study hall the next day.

"Promise not to tell?"

"Promise!" The girls were wearing matching French berets and dangling earrings. Their phase *Francaise* would last another week. Cowboy boots were next. Angelica's fashion choices always worked better on herself. Her bangs framed her beret perfectly, whereas Raelyn's black cap didn't do much for her caramel skin, frizzy head, and glasses that morning.

She leaned in slightly. "It's from Gil Richmond."

"Ugh!" Angelica made a face, one eyebrow up, the other down. Her shoulder created a barrier between them, as if Raelyn had contracted germs. "*That* ego head?"

"So what? He's just a boy."

"Yeah, but *Gil Richmond?*" Angelica teased.

Okay, did you miss it? For once in her life, Raelyn was first at *something.* She knew for a fact that Angelica had never received a love letter. This was the support she got from her best friend. "Whatever," she confided, a giggle under her breath. They assembled notebooks on the table.

They had become friends as kindergarten bus buddies. They

lived two miles apart but in different worlds. Angelica's family was exotic. Her father was in law enforcement and always looked regal in his pressed dark blue suits and shaped hat with the gold insignia. Her mother was an opera singer with voluptuous red hair, porcelain skin, and large blue eyes. She traveled often, and Angelica went with her to places like Kansas City, Toronto, Miami, and Colorado Springs. Portraits hung throughout their house of her mother in elegant costumes posing, presumably, on stages all over the world. She'd always promised that one day they'd take Raelyn to the opera and she could experience the magic herself. Between that and going to church every Sunday, Angelica had a closet full of lovely dresses.

Raelyn's parents were mortifying. Her mother wore a shower cap on her head at work—no lie—and rubber gloves, booties over her sneakers and cotton scrubs. She was an emergency room nurse with blood-and-guts stories. Her father wore the daily, boring basics: *slacks*, collared shirt, and embarrassing *loafers*. Whether at the community college where he worked, or at weekly legislature meetings, he always looked exactly the same.

In the Quinn family, Angelica was everything. If she wanted art lessons, she got art lessons. Music, dance, pottery, sailing lessons—you name it, she got it. High marks, excellent reviews, praise, praise, praise, and admittedly all well deserved. Raelyn, on the other hand, lived in the shadows of her troublesome big brother, who in the past year had zapped the energy right out of the house. When Angelica was three, her father had built her the most awesome playhouse. It was sculpted from clay and straw, with two round windows as eyes on either side of an arched door, and hair atop the roof growing grass and flowers. The inside was a cheery cave with built-in, curvy seats and a polka-dot ceiling. *Happy Hollow* made everything that happened there enchanting.

Once, when they were new friends and playing inside *Happy Hollow*, Raelyn had confided in her about the Glitter. Angie had looked at her oddly. "Glitter? What glitter?"

"You know, the *Glitter*. At bedtime. Before you fall asleep."

But Angelica had remained blank. "I don't know what you're talking about."

"You mean, you don't see the Glitter?" Raelyn had assumed everybody saw it.

When she hopped on the bus the next morning, she'd been met by Angelica's loud greeting for all to hear: "Hi, Glitter Girl!" leaving Raelyn speechless. After several days of this, she'd finally blurted, "Can you not?" She followed with a weak laugh. "That was a secret just between us."

"Oh, I didn't know!" Angelica had winced as if she'd just sipped lemonade without sugar. "I'm sorry." Then an ingenious idea had crossed her mind. "I'll call you G-G for short. No one will ever know. How's that?" Angelica was a natural problem solver.

And that is how the nickname Gigi came to be.

Raelyn was now on the fifth math problem. "Anj," she whispered, "did you hear about Blundertown Park?"

". . . No. What about it?"

"Dogs aren't allowed there anymore. Or in *any* park. I know because I took Penny yesterday, and there's a sign."

"Really? Oh, that's too bad," Angie whispered back. She switched notebooks. "Want to compare answers?" She would catch right up to Raelyn in no time. She was a straight-A student and just plain smart at everything. Even in science, where Raelyn excelled, Angelica excelled just a little bit more. They compared answers to the first several problems, and Rae fixed a careless arithmetic error.

When they got to number seven, Raelyn whispered, "This is a weird one."

"How?"

She read the problem in a low voice: "Facts: price of gasoline: $3.47 per gallon; vans travel at 28 miles per gallon; county dog population: 476. Question: If 24 county vans travel a combined 2,750 miles to transport all of the dogs across the border, how much would it cost the county to become completely dog-free?"

Angelica punched numbers on her calculator. "The answer is $340.80."

"But don't you think it's weird?" The girls looked at each other.

Angie explained, "They try to trick you to think it's harder than it is. You don't need the dog population at all to figure out the answer. You just calculate the gallons and then multiply by the cost: $340.80."

"But why would they be putting all those dogs in vans? Where would they be taking them?"

"Gigi," Angie laughed, still whispering, "it's just a math problem."

"I know, but it's, it's. . . ." she was staring at the open page in front of her. She wondered what Gil Richmond would think; he had a dog. But she'd never get the chance to ask.

"You're over thinking, Silly. You just apply the same formula as all the other problems, basically," she reasoned, but Rae had a glossed-over look in her eyes. "Hey. Earth to Gigi. It's just math!" She glanced over at Raelyn's notebook, where a string of letters—*GEGE, GEGE*—was penciled along the top of the page. "By the way," Angie pointed out, "Gigi is spelled *'Gigi,'* not *'Ge'*".

They continued working in silence. As study hall was about to end, Angelica asked about getting together over the weekend.

"I can't. We're going away."

"Oh. Where?"

"To my grandparents," Raelyn lied. The truth was they were going to visit her brother. It was no one else's business, and Jack's troubles sometimes created friction. Angelica's father was a cop, after all.

"Oh, darn." Angie crinkled her nose. "There's this new group tomorrow—a neighborhood 'Ollie' thing. I thought maybe we could go together." She pivoted on her chair and smiled. "But have fun!"

The bell sounded, and a flurry of movement instantly followed. It was called a "bell" for lack of another term. In fact, the piercing *bzzz* was anything but a pleasant jingle. It buzzed thirteen times a day, and everyone—students, teachers, administrators—responded like robots.

The girls dodged their way through the packed hallway with their good friends, Megan and Cierra. Before they reached the intersection to part ways for next class, they spotted Gil Richmond among the masses. He bounced through the halls as if he had small springs in the tips of his sneakers, shaking the hair from his brow. Angie ribbed Rae softly and smiled. "See you later, Gigi." She formed a heart shape with her fingers and thumbs. Raelyn flashed the same back. She caught the last glimpse of his head bobbing down Corridor B until it blurred out of sight.

It had been years since she'd thought about that kindergarten bus ride when the heart-shaped sign was born. Angie'd had the window seat, as always. Gil Richmond was across the aisle with a boy named Cody. No sooner had they arrived at Cody's stop and Gil was alone, he peed his pants. Raelyn had instinctively known from his ghost-white profile and the dark spot that appeared on his lap. He'd looked ready to cry.

Angie had peeked over her. "What are you looking at?"

"Nothing." Raelyn must have been gawking. She'd turned away from Gil and scooted forward to block Angie's view. When they reached her stop, she'd said, "Hey, look for me out the window."

"Why?"

"I'll—I'll give you a sign."

"A *friendship* sign?" Angelica had squealed.

"Um, yeah."

"Okay!"

"Start looking now, and keep looking."

As Angie did that, Raelyn had tossed her brand-new sweatshirt onto Gil's lap and pressed her finger to her lips without looking at him. She'd hurried off the bus. Angie had turned squarely away, fixated on the window pane.

Once she'd spotted Angie in the window, Raelyn joined her thumbs and curved fingers in clumsy pantomime, forming what they both knew was intended to be a heart shape. Angie, gleaming, had instantly mimicked the sign back, an imperfect heart against the smudged window. This would remain their friendship sign for years to come. But only Raelyn knew that, in truth, it had not been born out of their friendship at all.

THE MOTHERS WERE CURIOUS. Gil Richmond's mom would ask whose sweatshirt was in the laundry, but he would never tell. When Rae explained to her mother that she'd lost her new hoodie at school, her mother had written a note for the teacher. Two days later, the sweatshirt had appeared in the Lost and Found box. Ms. Gibble had given it to Raelyn, folded and fluffy with scented fabric softener.

There were only two people in the world who knew that this sweatshirt was forever tainted with a boy's pee. That was never going to change. Rae had stuffed the sweatshirt in the trash bin just before mounting the bus home. As far as her mother would ever know, the sweatshirt had been Lost but not Found. She and Gil didn't look at each other for the rest of their kindergarten year, but she'd never told anyone about it. Not even Angelica.

CHAPTER 4

Strange Trip To The Vending Machines

I DREAMED WE WERE VISITING *a distant aunt and uncle who in real life don't exist.* "Now, listen up, both of you," Dad *lectured but looked directly at Jackson, who was thirteen at the time.* "They are very strict. You must not, under any circumstances, leave the sofa without permission from our hosts. Is that understood?"

Jack said, "That's retarded. Why?"

Mom chimed in, "it's a House Rule. Your father and I can't do anything about it."

My brother challenged her. "Can we jump on the couch?"

"Yes."

"Can we do flips on it?"

"Yes."

"So we can do anything *on it, we just can't get off it?*"

"Correct."

"That's retarded."

Mom added, "If your foot so much as touches the floor, there'll be serious consequences."

"Like what?" Jack asked.

"You don't want to know, children. Just do as we say," she warned.

We were welcomed into their lovely home, a crystal chandelier flitting prisms all about. They were all smiles, and you never would have guessed the evil menace beneath the surface. "Have a seat on The Sofa!" Aunt exclaimed. I immediately climbed onto the oversized couch and extended my legs straight out, sharks ready to nibble my toes if they dangled too closely. I was terrified, Jack much less so; he sank next to me and started jumping and flipping about, a huge commotion to my left. I glared at him with panicked eyes, but his were laughing. The adults visited at the far end of the room.

The next thing I knew, two sneakers were planted solidly on the carpet next to me.

"Jackson!" our mother shrieked. She instantly clasped both hands over her mouth, but it was too late. The room fell silent, with five sets of eyes on him.

"Jackson," Uncle called as if discovering an acquaintance from across a banquet hall. He approached with Aunt gracefully at his side. "Come along with us!" They whisked him away. Time passed. I asked my father what had happened, but he only looked down. Finally, the door swung open and in walked Uncle carrying my brother. Jack was smaller than usual and had a wide grin. His hair was combed neatly with a part in the middle—not *the way he ever wore it.*

"Jack?" I called out quietly. A smile remained fixed on his chiseled face, and I realized he was not my brother any more. His teeth were too white. His cheeks were made of paint. Uncle held two dowels over his head with tiny strings attached to my brother's wrists and ankles. When he maneuvered the rods in one direction, the mini left arm and right leg lifted, bending at the knee and elbow. When the rod was tipped the other way, the opposite appendages moved. He was dancing to the commands of the strings.

Jack had been made into a puppet.

IT WAS VISITING DAY. Though she wouldn't admit it, Raelyn missed her brother Jackson. But she didn't like the long drive, the security lines and cumbersome rules, and, worst of all, the gagging smells of the cafeteria.

The Devines sat at the small, assigned table in the food hall, each occupying one of the sides and leaving the fourth side (facing the guards) for Jackson. Ms. Devine's lips were pressed tight. Rae and her brother always insisted she looked like a bird. Her eyes were deep-set and close together, and her nose was small, pointy, and narrow. She even walked like a bird at times, in hurried, purposeful jerks, and her middle name was Robin. (The parents denied this resemblance.) Jackson had inherited Joan Robin's hazel eyes and smooth hair but looked nothing like a bird. Girls went nuts over him. His skin was the color of chocolate milk. Rae had their father's dark eyes, and her complexion was a deeper blend than her brother's.

Joan Robin pulled a few anti-bacterial wipes from her purse and handed them to husband and daughter. "Rae, dear, wash your hands," she said. She wiped every inch of the table and used another to disinfect her hands. Then she sat, straight as a pin in her black and white, arms folded in her lap. Rae watched her own legs move in tangled circles below, never catching up with each other. Dad was eyeing the far corner of the room. They waited in separate silence.

"Here he is." He stood up.

Jackson approached from the opposite entrance, wearing a serious, adult expression. But when he saw them, he flashed a huge smile, and Raelyn recognized her familiar big brother again. His longish, wavy hair had been cut like everyone else's there, clearing the forehead and the ears with a crisp edge, with no hair at the nape. He looked handsome in his dark gray belted trousers and buttoned shirt, tucked in. He'd grown some muscles. This might be where he grows up, she thought. Their parents were hoping the same thing.

They were permitted a single embrace, and that was it. The remainder of the visit would be from these seats, no touching. Such was this strange and unwelcoming place known as Juvie Jail.

"Hi, Jackass," Rae gloated.

("Raelyn!" exclaimed Mom).

Jackson laughed. "So I take it you got my first two clues."

"G and an E," Rae answered proudly.

"Not bad, Baby Rae. Hey, Dad. . . ." He was already eyeing the rows of vending machines.

But Raelyn was mystified. "How could you remember what someone wrote on the bus a hundred years ago?"

He tapped his brain three times. "I remember everything. I know who loves Marcus, who hates history, who sucks—"

"Jackson!" exclaimed Mom.

". . .At spelling, *Mom*," he said, then turned back to his sister. "Photographic memory." His sleeves were rolled up just enough to show a black-ink tattoo on his left forearm. It was a compass with *North* pointing toward his bulging triceps. "Hey, Dad," he repeated, "can you get me a slice of pizza? And an ice cream bar. Oh, and a Snickers?"

"You bet." Dad was fanning the stack of singles in front of him. "How about you?" he asked Rae.

"I'm coming!" She jumped up and followed him to the Wall of Vending Machines, stocked with packaged items pretending to be food. There were candy bars with "real chocolate flavoring," and Styrofoam cups with freeze-dried noodles and powder: just add hot water by pressing a button. There were sodas, chips, and ice cream.

The kids loved the place!

The cafeteria had filled up with visitors and residents all seated in the same way, with the boy in trouble facing front. Every boy from high school could be there. Voices bounced off the walls, a generic, high-decibel loudness.

"Thanks, Dad." His eyes grew big as he bit into his slice as if it were prime rib. It didn't get any better than that there—food and family. "What's new, Rae?" It had been a while. Specifically, Raelyn did not tell him about Gil Richmond's love letter. Or her non-response, or the confusing predicament she found herself in over so-called romance. She did tell him about softball next spring, and that she and her friends were still undecided about what to wear for Halloween. "That's good, that's good," he replied, as if being un-costumed with only ten days left was good. He tore off the wrapper of his candy bar. "How's Little Penny?"

"Jack!" she exclaimed. "They don't let dogs in the parks anymore!"

"What? What do you mean, they don't let dogs in the park? Of *course* they do." He twisted up into his goofy face.

"She's right." Their father's voice was low.

"What? What's up with that?"

Mr. Devine proceeded to tell Jackson the same thing in the same way he had told the others over dinner, but in more boring detail: dog poop, skyrocketing taxes, inflation. Foreclosed homes, HR, PD, drone, drone, chugga-chugga, train on tracks, heavy with cargo. The other three rolled their eyes and sighed, sorry he'd asked.

Like Raelyn, Jackson also had a special relationship with Penelope. In fact, he was the one who had taught her how to spell, even though his little sister got all the credit. When Raelyn was eight, she began her 4-H oral presentation this way: "Penelope is a very smart dog. She can even spell. Don't believe me? (*Coy smile at the judges.*) Watch this." She called to Penny, sitting ten feet away: "T-R-E-A-T!" Penelope trotted instantly to her and caught the treat with customary grace. The judges were impressed. The Rae and Penelope team earned their way to the State competition.

The State venue was larger. The judges were better dressed, the competition more cut-throat. And, unfortunately, Penelope was ill and woozy from medicine. Raelyn's parents tried to convince her to give it up. The only thing more traumatic than failing in public was watching your child fail in public.

But if Rae had faith in anything, it was in her Penelope. She was bent on a miracle and crossed her fingers, an auditorium of eyes watching. She spelled the magic word. Penelope lay motionless. "T-R-E-A-T," she called again. Not a muscle. After a third futile spelling, she popped an unearned biscuit in the dog's mouth.

The second dog feat had been equally disastrous. She recalled her mother in the second row with a nail biting, pointy smile and a plea in her eye, her father's slow, even nod. Jackson sat next to them, giggling up at her, his silver braces flashing. After that she remembered nothing. But apparently, she ad-libbed to the panel for the full three minutes while stroking Penelope in her lap, and even bowed in the end. The Rae and Penny team earned high "sympathy" scores. The comments: *You rose to a difficult challenge,*" "*You could have quit, but you didn't,*" "*Ninety percent of life is showing up.*" Two days later, Penelope had returned to normal again. Timing was everything. The story had become Devine family lore, Jackson's teaching skills all but forgotten.

By the next visit with Jackson two weeks later, more anti-dog rules had been imposed. Raelyn relished reporting because no one else would. "And Penny can't even be off leash *in our own yard.* Plus, we can only buy her a small amount of food every week. It's gotten super expensive. It's called a ration," she continued with an unscripted string of gossipy things to report.

"Hold up, hold up." He looked at his dad again. "Is this stuff true?"

"Hello! Duh," she protested. "I'm not some dumb little kid, Bozo! Why would I make it up?"

Mom weighed in, the voice of reason. "There are some new laws, that's all. Penny is fine—same as always." She said this to end the discussion. Then she added, with a chuckle to end it more light-heartedly, "She needed to lose a little weight anyway, *pffh!*" Her jokes were never funny. Other than the hug, she hadn't shifted her posture one bit since they got there, hands still folded in her lap. "Did you read the books we sent you?"

"Yeah, yeah. They were good. Thanks, Mom." But he turned again to their father. "So what does being leashed have to do with taxes?"

"It's, uh, complex, I suppose."

But the more Raelyn reported, the more incredulous her brother became. "That's effing messed up, *yo!*"

"Jackson." Everyone knew that was Dad's way of scolding him for saying the "F" word in front of his little sister— even though he hadn't actually said the "F" word, and she wasn't little anymore, something they kept forgetting.

Mom added, "You know her flair for drama, Sweetie."

"I'm not exaggerating! It's true." Raelyn's cheeks flared deep crimson. "And when we took Penny to Doc Goodman's for her annual checkup, it cost us *triple* because he has to pay all these new fees. He said Daffy County is trying to put him out of business." According to Doc, she was his best helper, with a unique, calming effect on Penelope. She had never missed an appointment.

"Raelyn, hush now," her mother said.

Rae looked to her dad for an unlikely hint of support, but he cleared his throat instead. "Yeah, that's enough." No help from Big Bad Brother, either.

She was fuming. They considered everything she said or did a tantrum because she was the youngest. How old did she have to be, thirteen? Sixteen? A hundred eighty? She threw herself back into her chair and crossed her arms in a demonstrative huff. She sank down, down, down, until her eyebrows were level with the table, a blanket of hair flung over her face. That's exactly where she would stay until visiting hours were over.

Her brother looked from one to the other. "Whatever, that's effing messed up."

Okay, back up. Did you miss that? He ignored the scolding he'd *just* received over using the "F" non-word, and the parents ho-hummed right past it. Messed up, anyone?

"Well, I'm not political," Mom said decidedly. "It is what it is. I always say, you don't have to like it, but it *is* the law."

"I agree," Father nodded.

"Yep, I agree, too. Absolutely." Jackson nodded. "You *do* always say that, Mom."

"So how's everything going, son?" Strategic change of subject by Dad.

Jackson began rattling off lofty calculations of weeks and months, concluding that he'd be out before his seventeenth birthday. Six months.

"So have you made any, you know, friends?"

"Mom." He put on his special brand of charm. "That's a no-win question. You know that, right?" he explained with a half-smile. "If I say no, I haven't made any friends, you'll worry about my social skills and that I'm lonely. Right or wrong?" She nodded slightly, conceding. "If I say yes, I've made friends *here*, you'll have a heart attack."

Rae burst out laughing. He was pretty hilarious.

Then the real question: "Have some of your programs helped?" Mom was referring, of course, to substance abuse treatment without saying so. No one ever talked directly to Raelyn about these things, but it was obvious. Not to mention, she often eavesdropped on nighttime conversations from half way down the stairs.

"Yeah, Mom, they have," he assured. "Don't worry. I won't be back here. Ever. Promise." He held out his pinky finger, and she locked hers around it with a cautious smile. A pinky promise with her beloved first-born.

They took turns with updates. Dad grumbled about the colossal mess the legislature was facing. But his voice lit up when he spoke of his new software program at the college, color returning to his drained face. Mom had ordered an emergency air lift for a bleeding child—a victim of a head-on collision. She sometimes accompanied the victims in the helicopter on their way to the expansive city hospital. Raelyn always wanted just once in her life to fly with her mother in the helicopter! But, of course, it wasn't allowed. She could lose her job.

Rae's posture had accidentally returned to normal. She remarked how stupid it was to play badminton in gym class. How could you get a *grade* in badminton? Why was it called a birdie when it looked nothing like a bird?

"Chirp, chirp," Jackson cooed beneath the radar (an inside, Mom-joke). Rae covered her giggle with full hands. The folks didn't let on.

Attention, Inmates. The loudspeaker announced. *Roll call.* Chairs skidded everywhere, and the teenage boy in gray at each table stood at attention. The place grew completely silent. By the time the process was completed, visiting hours were nearly over.

As much as the parents wished he wouldn't, Jackson brought the parting conversation back to Penelope. "If I was out there, I'd be on the streets protesting! I'd make sure my voice was heard." He made a valiant fist, his tattoo bumpy from veins and muscles.

"But you're not," his mother reminded him. Suddenly, she shook her head as if dodging a buzzing fly. "Oh, I am so *sick* of hearing about it. The Dogs this, and The Dogs that. It's all a bunch of nonsense if you ask me. I just wish it would end already."

"This will pass," their father said, hoping it was true. "Before you know it, everything will be back to normal."

They used up their allotment of goodbye hugs. Jack hugged his sister's bony shoulders and kissed her on the cheek. "Take care of our Penelope for me." He looked into her eyes in a deliberate way, a telepathic way, as if they shared a secret pact. She tried to mimic the look back to him but wasn't sure how. Or exactly why. Just before he turned to leave, he added, "I'll send you my third clue next week." Then he lifted his chin the way he always did when he was acting cool.

That was it until next time.

CHAPTER 5

There Goes The Neighborhood!

THIS DREAM WAS ONLY A FEW SECONDS LONG. *Earlier that evening we'd carved the annual Devine jack-o'-lantern. It was an artsy composite: my amateur sketch of the mouth, Jack's drawing of the eyes, Mom's crest for a nose, and Dad's squiggly markings suggesting ears. But in my dream, the facial features began to rearrange themselves. I stared as the feral gourd mutated from one face to another, an ever-changing cast of characters on its curved, waxy surface. Next to me, Jack mimicked the expressions—first goofy, then pouty, then sinister. I dove into the safe hollow of his chest.*

THERE WAS AN IMPATIENT BANGING at the front door, angry knuckles on oak.

"Someone's at the door!" Penelope barked, barreling toward the foyer. *"Coming! Be right there!"* Rae followed. It was the neighbor, Kelly Davis. Rae greeted her, and Penelope sat angelically at her

side, tail sweeping in anticipation. But there was no treat for her. Both Devines knew instantly that something was wrong. "Is your mother or father home?" Her coral lips were pinched.

"No." Ms. Davis knew that. They were still at work. She rarely appeared at their door except to sell a raffle ticket for some cause or other. But that day her hands were empty, fidgeting to fend off the late November air.

"Well, let them know I stopped by." Her puffs of breath reminded Rae of a dragon hurling fire. She was winded just from walking up the road.

"Should I tell them what it's about?"

"Well, your *dog* pooped in front of my yard," she reported in a clipped, uncharacteristic tone. Dark roots cut a rigid line on either side of her part. "It's still there. And I don't like it."

Rude much, Rae noted. It was then that she spotted the armband on the woman's jacket. It was wide and orange, with black letters: *ON!*—short for the *Ollie's Neighborhood* watch group, which had become quite popular of late. "Should I go pick it up?"

"If you don't mind." Ms. Davis may as well have said, "That's an order." A crease appeared above her over-plucked brow. "We can't afford any trouble, Philip and I. If you know what I mean." No, Rae didn't know. "And *it* was in your yard yesterday, too. It wasn't leashed." Her blue powder-puff eyes were icy.

Since when had Ms. Davis called Penny an "*it*"? She continued her know-it-all, bossy kind of lecture. "As your *ON!* representative, I could give you a ticket. But instead, I'm offering you a warning. As a courtesy."

It was no courtesy; it was a threat. This was official business. For the first time in her life, Raelyn took the next-door neighbor seriously. Penny's tail tucked inward.

The bright coral mouth back-pedaled into a phony smile. "Just a friendly reminder," Ms. Davis said as she winked at Raelyn.

Eww, why did grown-ups do that? Did they wink when they were kids, or was it a habit they acquired with maturity? she wondered as she and Penelope followed the curve toward the Davis house. The about-face was unnerving. Just a couple weeks before, Ms. Davis had presented a treat from her pocket and patted Penelope on the nose, as she had done for years. Why such ruffling of feathers in their ordinarily superficial neighbor? The families weren't close—neither the parents nor the children, whose ages and milestones missed each other by years. The clans minded their own business and stayed away from touchy subjects (politics, race, landscaping, finances, religion, fitness, crime, and parenting). So they got along just fine.

Rae searched for the offensive pile, but didn't see anything. The closer to the Davis house they were, the lower to the ground Penelope sniffed. *Getting warmer,* she deduced as she followed sharp zig-zags with her nostrils. *Warmer, warmer. . .* her tail beating behind her. *Hot! Hotter! Found it!*

There it was: a tiny brown clump on the edge of the sidewalk, not much bigger than a buckeye.

Kelly Davis had come all the way over for *this*? This is what the neighbors were up in arms about? Raelyn didn't know whether to laugh or kick the little clump straight to the Davises' front door. Surely, this could be the product of anyone in the neighborhood. Why pin it on us—why not Boxer, or that yappy terrier with the crooked ear?

Not mine, Penelope concluded. *Definitely Boxer.*

Raelyn scooped it up with her baggie-gloved hand. Come to think of it, she hadn't seen either of them lately. She hadn't seen Prince for weeks. She still hadn't responded to Gil Richmond's love letter, if you could call it that. Each time she tried, she found herself up against the same dilemma: She couldn't say yes, and she didn't want to say no. A "date" (assuming) at the park with their dogs was impossible. Did that cancel his offer? What did he see in her, anyway—not that he did. These thoughts had buzzed around her for five weeks and two days. . .but who was counting?

Jackson's third clue crossed her mind. All this time she could have been multi-tasking and searching for the answer along with the poop. She studied the front porches along the way, stopping at the foot of each for a better view. The third clue went like this:

> *Did I see a smile beneath your frown*
> *Even though I've let you down?*
> *I wish I knew.*
> *Well, here's my third clue:*

A lady's fine porch display
For many years and a day
Needs neither sunshine nor water
Whether cold or much hotter—
These blossoms are here to stay.

So far, she'd spotted no flowers. Rae and Penny found themselves at the entrance to Blundertown Park, where the unfortunate sign was still posted. They both looked longingly into the field, the jungle gym, and the lonely baseball diamond. Penelope's tail wagged.

"No, we can't go in there, Penny," she explained.

They stared at each other for a few moments—one set of charcoal eyes steadfast on the other. When nothing happened, Penny barked politely, *"I'd like to go in."*

"We can't go in. I'm sorry."

"Do let me in, please," Penelope graciously repeated, then added for extra flair, *"this minute."*

"Not today, Penny. Come on," Rae tugged on the leash.

Penny dug in her heels with poised determination. They continued the push-pull dance for a few moments, but in the end, of course, Raelyn won. That was the way of things in the pack. But she was not pleased.

You see, it wasn't lost on Penny that they hadn't been to the park in ages. The stroll always started predictably enough: past her Special Neighbor's house, the pond where the white creatures floated mysteriously across the surface, past the home of the deranged felines. But instead of turning into the park, why, they'd walk straight past it. Eventually, they'd turn toward home, a random one-eighty at Rae's discretion. It was hardly fair, but again, what could she do? It was all very curious.

She was trotting alongside Raelyn when an ominous tickle spread across her nose. She tried scratching it. She swatted again several times while trying at the same time to keep up. This reduced her to a graceless gait—a humiliating, three-legged hop. The tormenting itch spread across her muzzle, flews, and cheeks. She swatted frantically to no avail.

"What's the matter, My Lady? C'mon." Rae scratched all over Penny's face and coaxed her along.

It was precisely the relief Penelope needed, and she refocused and found her pace. There was always next time. Perhaps then she would meet up with old friends in the park, get all the most recent gossip. She was not nosy, mind you; she was far classier than that. She merely liked to keep current. How she missed the park! It was her most exciting destination most days. One never knew who might be there: her dear friend Prince; or Oscar, Nolia, or Abby; or the people who were so friendly! Even when it was empty, the park was a happening place. She would sniff daintily around her familiar stomping ground—the spilled ice cream spot, the sweaty scents around the baby swings, the leftover specks under the picnic tables. Or discover new signs of old acquaintances, the unique fingerprint of the canine species: No two dogs' pee smelled exactly alike. This sleuthing activity not only kept the mind sharp and useful, it was one of her favorites. Who'd been at the park of late, whom might she have missed—the proof was in the pee.

She also enjoyed her Matching Game at the park. Over the years, she'd become quite skilled at it. The tiny pebble droppings came from the four-leggeds whose babies wore precious white spots. What a surprise to discover (by acute skill and sensory perception) that the long, squishy specimen came from the graceful water floaters, the runny white stuff from the bickering creatures overhead, and the clumps from those nasty competitor types. Again, the samples she most enjoyed exploring at the park were from her own species—Boxer, Prince, that intolerable, chatty terrier. These samples were a real bonanza, since they were typically scooped up on contact.

It might not seem like much. But she had enjoyed these activities her entire life and she looked forward to them. Now they had been yanked away for no particular reason. And her friends had all but disappeared—not a hint of them anywhere.

Penelope noticed the obvious signs: the darkening world, the deepening chill, the smell of thunder. Just as she had predicted, a few drops of sleet sliced through the sky. Within seconds, the tick-tick-ticking surrounded them. Rae pulled up her coat hood and turned abruptly toward home. Penny followed at her side.

Just ahead, the Millers' house was long overdue for a painting. A foreclosure sign had been stabbed into the brown lawn. Raelyn eyed the porch for the flower clue. The door opened and out came elderly, cheerless Mildred Miller, shivering in her knitted sweater. "You didn't take that mutt into the park, did you?" Her thin, menacing voice traveled down the steps and landed, an accusation, at Rae's feet.

"No."

"You better not. Filthy canine, it's all *his* fault." She yanked her cardigan close—a dramatic exclamation point!—and shuttered herself back into her paint-chipped home. Not a hello, isn't it a lovely day?

Talk about filthy. . .that stinky old sweater probably hadn't been washed in a hundred years. Old Mrs. Miller always wore it, even on hot summer days. She probably slept in it, too. Gross. Raelyn stuck her tongue out as they passed. Suddenly she was burning to know: why the pudgy, two-faced neighbor and the nasty old sweater lady? Was everyone insane? Why the exclusion of her dear Penelope, posted with twisted wire? Why the cruel laws, the accusations, the offensive math problems? Her rage burned, and the sheets of ice pelted.

As she trudged along, it dawned on her that perhaps she was asking the wrong questions. Perhaps the answerable question was not why, but *who*: Who was behind all of this? The answer came to her instantly, like Penny's rubber ball bobbing to the surface of the lake.

Surely, the man behind it all was none other than Mr. Pumpkin Head.

Ollie Jerkins had a perfectly round, red-orange face. His head even had a few ruts like real pumpkins, and his cow-licked hair could be the stem. He was the Chief Executive of Daffy

County. Her father occasionally shared stories about him over dinner—all in fun, of course. ("What is said at the dinner table stays at the dinner table," he'd make them promise). She could picture all the players at the meetings, including the boss who insisted on the title "Chief Jerkins." But she and Jack had nicknamed him Mr. Pumpkin Head.

Not to mention, Mr. Pumpkin Head was hard to miss these days. Everyone in school knew who he was. He had spoken recently at a pep rally in the gym. By the time he finished, the students had felt a surge of loyalty to their school and community and tremendous self-pride, though they'd barely understood what he said. His voice was booming, his face tomato red. Listening to him, Rae had felt both exhilarated and terrified. But when he shared his life-changing story of his youth, she was decidedly not a fan. He had been bitten by a dog and hated dogs ever since. A tirade had followed about canines being dangerous and dirty, and that kids everywhere deserved cleaner neighborhoods. Then on to the ribbon cutting of the *Ollie's Kids Club,* which he was visiting every school to promote. Students had flocked to the table to sign up and grab an orange *OK!* armband. Angelica had been among them.

"Angie," Rae had called out, struggling to keep up with her, "what are you doing?" They both were in Chinese flats and faux silk kimonos.

"What? I want one of those arm thingies."

"Why? Don't go up there." But Angie had continued to follow, darting artfully among her peers to reach the table. She'd scribbled her name on the list and, with a triumphant smile, snatched an orange band. Rae had stood speechless a few feet away.

"Yeah, we've all heard Ollie's boyhood trauma," her father had mused later that evening, his arms spread-eagled behind his neck, his feet on the coffee table. "His embellishments grow every day. Last week he told the Women's Auxiliary he needed fifty stitches and suffered permanent damage to his right calf. He blamed some dog *thirty years ago* for not getting a football scholarship in college," he had laughed. "It was eight stitches. And he's not athletic, that's all."

Her mother had shaken her head, amused. "You'd never guess Ollie was a victim the way he carries on, all fire and brimstone. He's a persuasive speaker, I'll give him that." She turned to the TV, top of the hour. "Quite a dog fetish, that man."

"Well, I don't like him," Rae had announced.

"You don't have to," her father had sighed wistfully. "He's not your boss. Lord knows I wish he weren't mine."

RAE AND PENNY CLIMBED THE HILL, the storm chasing at their heels. Newspaper headlines loomed before her, all pointing to Mr. Pumpkin Head. She'd been doing a little research lately. She was only eleven, but the web search was simple: just type in dog and *Ollie's Daily*, the local newspaper, formerly known as *The People's Daily*. A list of articles instantly appeared, and Mr. Pumpkin Head's fingerprints were all over them. Six weeks ago, a little article on page 23 read "Dog Terrorizes Child." According to the story, an eight-year-old boy had been frightened by a Chihuahua on Front Street while walking home from school on October 7. The boy hadn't been injured, and the dog's owner had quickly secured the pooch and been ticketed, according to Chief Ollie Jerkins. Two weeks later, on page 15, an article called, "County to Lassie: Go Home!" had discussed the municipal park ban:

> Our parks are green havens intended for social events and safe play for our youngsters," says Chief Ollie Jerkins, who supports the ban. "Not as dumping grounds from the bowels of dogs. It's time to end the filth and terror brought on by growling canines at the expense of our peaceful communities. Dog owners are subject to a $50.00 fine per violation.

So her father's explanation of the ban—the fiscal need to cut jobs—hadn't been wholly accurate.

A week later, on page 8, "Dog Curfew in Effect" reported that Chief Jerkins had responded to residents' complaints of barking with a five o'clock curfew. He directed citizens to call CAN-INES immediately upon the sighting of any dog after hours, or upon suspicion of such a sighting. The next day, on page 4, "Couple Arrested for Violating One Dog Rule" reported that Rick and Rita Smith had been charged with a felony for failing to turn over their "baggage" dog to County Hall. Failure to report a suspected violation was a "misdemeanor." The terminology sounded dire.

Had Raelyn's search included the term "canine," a recent front-page article would have appeared: *Wild Pack Of Canines Attacks Innocent Boy On Way Home From School.*

The incident had allegedly occurred on October 7 on Front Street—the same time and place as the minor incident previously reported. Somehow, the Chihuahua had evolved into a "wild pack," and the boy had suffered life-threatening injuries. Other recent news articles would have appeared, as well, with front-page headlines:

Filthy Canines Cause Public Health Disaster
Daffy's Economic Woes: Canines To Blame!
Jerkins: Urgent Action Needed To Curb Canine Population

Raelyn's key was in the door. She didn't remember taking it out of her pocket. She hadn't noticed the ice turn to pellets the size of grapes or her mother's car in the driveway either. Nor had she discovered any blossoms on porches.

Indoors, Penelope shook herself dry with a flurry of speed and precision. The Alpha Mother whisked slivers of ice from Rae's jacket. "Goodness, Raelyn," she exclaimed. "What in heaven's name are you doing out in *this*?" She was the boss of the family, the leader of the pack. *Allow me to help,* Penny offered and dutifully lapped up the frosty chips from the floor in the nick of time, preventing a puddled mess. Alpha ignored her, didn't even say hello. In the past, she used to scratch her under the chin each day with a cheerful, "Good morning, My Lady!" But not so lately. Sheer rejection. Only after Penelope pestered at her heels would she bend down and say, "Okay, okay," and give her a mindless flick along the back.

How topsy-turvy Penny's life had become. It was more than just the park. Her name came up with such frequency that she'd become a household celebrity of sorts. Except that each time it did, Rae cried or carried on so! Her hugs had always been a bit smothering, sweet thing, but now they were a choke hold around the chest and withers. It was as if the girl clung on for dear life. Penelope felt compelled to check on her through the night, stealing upstairs to her post at the side of the bed. Some rules must be broken, you see; the poor dear needed her. The father was the only one who seemed the same. He tossed a stick in the yard with the same speed, distance, and direction and for the same, too-brief period of time. But make no mistake: He was stiffing her on dinner. Did he take her for such a fool that he thought she wouldn't notice?

Was it something she'd done? she wondered. Had she offended in some way? The list was growing: her Favorite Neighbor, Alpha, Father, Prince, Boxer. They'd all deserted her in some fashion. Even grandmother—don't think for a minute she hadn't noticed. She smelled the proof when the family returned the other day: turkey, cinnamon, and cranberry. Penny had always taken such pride in her impeccable manners at Grandmother's. But this time she hadn't even been invited, imagine that! Penelope had never been so insulted in her life. Her ears drooped just thinking about it. *But who cares about a few petty snubs, anyway? Some people are ever so shallow.*

She retreated to her lonely spot under the desk when it occurred to her: The moment when it all began. It was that peculiar morning when the mail came twice. She remembered it all too well. She was tending to her chores in the empty castle. She didn't work out of the home like the rest of the family, but her job was no less important—even now that she was a respectable old lady. As always, the first thing she did when the family left for the day was tidy up the house. That morning there had been a dot of jelly on the table and a few pieces of cereal on Raelyn's chair.

That's when she heard that darn squeaky noise from the front door chute where the mail entered the house each day. How bold, the mail! Such an intrusion into the family's private sanctuary, one of her daily annoyances. But on that day, it was earlier than usual, and only a single piece of paper rather than the regular bundle. She inspected it most thoroughly. Then, of course, the propane man had come, that brazen intruder who barged across the lawn once a month with his ferocious hose. She threatened him through the window: *"Not an inch closer! I'm warning you!"* But he'd approached unabashed and smiled right at her. The nerve! Never trust a common trespasser. She had finally settled into her morning beauty rest when those God-awful, squeaky hinges interrupted her again. This time it really *had* been the mail. Twice in one day. . .strange indeed. A sliver of foreboding had pricked at the back of her neck. The last time the mail came twice, it had been about the boy, Jackson. Shortly afterward, he'd been gone. Who might it be this time? She had felt a sudden, desperate need to rearrange things in the house, something she hadn't done in ages. And like a frivolous young girl, she had.

Later that day, she and Raelyn had returned from the park for the first time without entering. Things hadn't been the same since.

THE CHILLY ODORS FROM THE STORM lingered in the kitchen. Penelope was alone. Oh, how she missed her old life and wondered when things would return to normal. Or was this the new normal? Again, her nerves got the best of her, and she searched for something harmless to rearrange. She spotted the kitchen towel over the oven door, the family's vulgar habit that irked her so. She gently pulled it down, fluffed it up until it was just so, and deposited it in the center of the room. *All is well,* she assured herself, returning to her spot. *Surely, it's nothing.* At times like this, mindless, repetitive activity could be therapeutic. It reduced anxiety simply by redirecting the energy. *Paws,* she decided—*I will lick my paws.* She massaged her arms in long caresses, one after another until her fur was silken, wet and relaxed. Still she stroked over and over, over and over. *Calm down. All is well.*

Suddenly, Alpha clip-clopped into the kitchen. "Damn it, Penelope. Again?" She whisked the towel off the floor and flicked it in Penny's face.

CHAPTER 6

A Single Vote

I DREAMED I WAS WALKING *into our living room and found both my parents on the sofa. But it was only their heads— nothing appeared below their necks. They were chatting away as if everything was normal.*

"Mommy! Daddy!" I screamed. "Your bodies are missing!" They smiled at me, unfazed. "You're just talking Bobble Heads!" I cried in disbelief. They acknowledged they knew this. In a way, it was funny to see their expressive heads chattering about, turning and cocking the way heads attached to bodies typically do. But in another way, it wasn't funny at all.

THERE WAS MUCH ABOUT MR. PUMPKIN HEAD that even Raelyn's father didn't know.

How Ollie Jerkins became Chief Executive was a wonder to everyone except himself. No superior intellect, skill, wealth, or family connection explained it. To the contrary, up to this point in his life, he had been a complete failure. He flunked out of college and ran several small businesses into the ground. He was terribly uncoordinated, never kept a girlfriend, had no rhythm, and couldn't carry a tune. In the beginning, his peculiar hatred for dogs earned him names like crackpot, maniac, and wacko. He distributed a pathetic, rambling poem degrading all canines, which people folded into paper airplanes and aimed back at his head on the streets. He was the butt of countless jokes.

But never say never, because Ollie kept at it. His presence at the right place and time was uncanny. And most importantly, he had an obsessive passion, no matter how absurd. Once he developed his craft and talking points, he spewed his crazy talk nonstop. He hooked enough voters to get him elected to his first political position, the new mayor of Blundertown.

At first, he was nothing more than that—small peanuts, small town. But in practice, both visibly and behind the scenes, he was an influential player in Daffy County politics, and a rising star. This gathering of clout between his broad shoulders had been four years in the works. There was no end in sight. Sure, there were discussions in basements with the lights low: How do we get rid of this guy? Whom can we groom, prep, and promote to beat him in the next election? There had been a few unsuccessful attempts; those candidates had been lucky to leave unscathed for fresh starts in distant towns.

Then one day, the front page of the *People's Daily* (it wasn't *Ollie's Daily* yet) announced in bold letters: "Mayor Jerkins Becomes New County Executive." His predecessor was an elderly man who had long lost his stomach for this kind of politics. He passed the baton to the ruddy-faced bully without a fight. And that is how Ollie became the head honcho of Daffy County, his hand in every pot, his signature on every dotted line.

But it still wasn't enough for him.

One of the things Raelyn's father never shared at the dinner table was the recent, secret vote on the Emergency Act. The Act would confer virtually unlimited powers on Chief Jerkins in the event of a so-called emergency. The Chief had given a fervent speech to the legislature on why it was necessary to pass the Act by a majority vote. The County was in the throes of deep crisis, he bellowed. His spittle reached the far side of the table when he spoke.

He wasn't a large man, but he could dominate a room. He sat at the helm of the long conference table with five council members on one side and four on the other. No one took the side opposite him. He knew he had it made when a roomful of people laughed at his jokes even he knew weren't funny. These were people he could make sweat (Rae's father, Vigil Devine, included). He could trigger nightmares that left no memorable trace in the morning. It was silly, they knew. After all, they were adults living in the USA, not in some dreadful place without elections and free speech. Yet these primitive power dynamics never really go away no matter where you are or how old you have become.

You may have heard of back-stabbing politicians: set-ups, deceit, nasty rumors, some of which are untrue. Local politics could be brutal, but not in Blundertown, where folks all got along, slapped each other's backs, and worked in harmony. And of course they laughed at Ollie's jokes—comic relief. On nearly all matters prior to this one, the vote would have been unanimous. They'd all go home with an evening respectably spent and a pittance well earned.

But the Emergency Act was different. When Chief Jerkins opened the floor for discussion, no one wanted to be the one to disagree. It was a challenging feat—how to praise and flatter but at the same time suggest that his ideas were crazy. It simply couldn't be done. Passing the Emergency Act would mean that Ollie, alone, could thereafter make any rule at all during an emergency. Yet the *definition* of emergency remained dangerously vague. In practice, couldn't anything be deemed an emergency? This went too far, even for some of the cowardly legislators. Naturally, no one said so.

However, when it came to voting, two "nays" were muttered almost instantly. Half way around the table, the vote was split: two "ayes" in favor and two "nays" against. The room was still. Every stomach churned. Vigil Devine studied the flushed faces of his colleagues who had already cast their votes. Then he studied the ghostlike faces of those who were next. He would be last, but his time was coming.

Three more votes tipped the balance in favor of the "nays." You could almost see the smoke coming out of Ollie's ears. The next vote tied it, four to four.

And then it was Vigil Devine's turn. His vote would seal the matter one way or the other. If he voted "aye," we had a dictator.

If he voted "nay," we didn't, but his own troubles would be just beginning. He could be his daughter's age right now, sitting in the sterile courtroom before the judge. He was expected to cast his vote for one, but not the other, of his divorcing parents. The helpless echo in his ears was the same. The hollows in his gut were the same. He never could do it then, and he wasn't sure he had it in him now. He swallowed hard. All eyes were diverted elsewhere except for Mr. Pumpkin Head's, who drilled their way into Vigil's dark, uneasy stare.

"I abstain," Vigil declared.

"You *what?*" Chief Jerkins boomed.

Vigil said, a little louder, "I choose not to vote. I abstain."

There were rustled exchanges around the table. Then Ollie's lips curled upward and his left dimple appeared. He pulled out the *Legislative Procedure Manual* from his inside jacket pocket. Who knew he kept it there? He thumb-flipped through the pages until he located what he was looking for, and read aloud: "*In the event of a tie vote, the County Executive breaks the tie.*"

Congratulations. Vigil had created a dictator.

IT TOOK A WEEK FOR HIM TO CONFIDE IN HIS WIFE. (He did so only partially.) It was nighttime, the time for adult discussions. He was distraught and rambling, elbows propped on the low table, chin in hands. "How can Ollie get away with this? We're not in Communist Russia. We live in the Sweet Land of Liberty, for Thee I Sing. Purple mountain majesties, checks and balances, the whole nine yards. He can't just strip the legislature of its power like this." But his last words rang hollow. He knew that he and his fellow council members had set the stage long before the Emergency Act. His forehead pounded his fists. "Joan, what do I do?"

"Well, dear, I think you're overreacting." Always the calm voice of reason. "Remember, we *are* in a state of emergency. I'm sure whatever Ollie does, it's to protect us all—the community." She stroked the dark curls above his ear. "Besides, once the emergency is under control, things will go back to normal."

"I hope you're right. I just feel like I ought to tell someone, file a. . .complaint or something." He paused. "I mean, people are being apprehended for things now that would never before—"

"Go over your boss's head? Lose your job? Over something as silly as *this?*" she said with a wave of her hand through the air. "That's your *Grand Plan* for the family?"

By then, Raelyn was straining to hear near the top of the stairs.

"I suppose you're right." Her father sat back, a hand on each giant knee. He gave a robust sigh as if blowing out candles. "We did follow the procedural manual." The pressure in his chest began to lift. "I suppose I should sleep on it, huh?"

Her mother smiled. "How did you know that's what I was going to say?"

"Oh, I don't know, just a hunch?"

"In the morning, this *mountain* will shrink back to the *tiny* ant hill that it *is*. Look," she said, her head peck-peck-pecking as she spoke, emphasizing select words, "*all* I want is to *keep* our *family safe*. To *teach* our *children* to be *good* human beings. Is *that* too much to ask?" He put his arm around her. Her lecture continued. "Choose your battles, Vigil. What's important is *our family*."

"Our family, Mom?" She was two-thirds down the staircase.

"Raelyn!" Her mother was startled. "What are you doing up?" (meaning, "How long have you been listening?")

"Look at our *family* albums. Penelope's everywhere. There's a whole photo album just of her," Rae's voice was rising. "How do we sign our New Year's cards? '*Peace. Vigil, Joan, Jackson, Raelyn*—" here she shouted—"*and Penelope Devine, 'Woof-woof!'*" Her nightgown formed a mini-tornado as she spun around and stomped back upstairs. A loud *thud!* followed as she tripped and banged her knee. "Ow!" she howled. "Don't laugh!" She slammed her bedroom door.

Penelope watched all of this unnoticed from her perch at the foot of the stairs. There she was again, the subject of another turbulent episode without the faintest idea why. All her life, she had prided herself in her ability to read the signs, interpret the clues, figure things out. Her skills were quite superior. She could tell, for instance, when her father was sad from the smell of the liquid in his glass, when Alpha was anxious from the increased pace of her footsteps around the kitchen. She could tell when her sister was keeping another secret from her extra glances when no one else was looking. Back when the dear boy was home (so fond of him—hadn't seen him in *ages!*), she alone foresaw trouble from the trail of subtle odors that followed him from the front door. Her two-legged family, wonderful though they were, had glaring deficiencies in the sensory department. They couldn't smell things the way she could, couldn't feel the vibrations or read between the lines. They were last to know a storm was approaching and rarely knew what time it was.

But now she was baffled, out of her league. The ways of the world, the rules of the road, everything had changed in some undefined way she couldn't grasp. The only things she knew for certain were: one, things were changing at an alarming rate and didn't look good for her; and two, Raelyn was in distress. She definitely would check on her again tonight.

CHAPTER 7

Doc Goodman's Frightful Night

THE NIGHT AFTER MY THIRD-GRADE *field trip to a glass-blowing exposition, I dreamed of the beautiful, molten-hot liquid expanding before me. Whether liquid or solid, glass could hurt you. At 1,800 degrees, it could burn a hole right through your heart; as a solid, it could slice you into pieces. Suddenly, the glowing mound exploded before my eyes into a solid burst of silver daggers. I huddled with Penelope in the corner as the particles came down like rain.*

WHEN RAELYN WAS NINE, Doc Goodman had dark wavy hair. When she was eleven, it had gone all white, a thick coat of snow on his tall head. He was quickly aging, but he was still the best veterinarian in Daffy County. He'd been named Best Vet for eight of the last ten years. If I were a dog, she thought, and had to be poked and pricked, prodded and restrained, if I had to be subjected to someone shoving a sharp instrument up my tush and inspecting my privates, I'd want that person to be Doc Goodman.

Penelope would agree. She had a love-hate relationship with her doctor, his staff, his waiting room, and the parking lot outside his office. She knew as soon as the car made the right-hand turn onto Chestnut Street. At nine, she had relieved herself the instant she entered the waiting room, surprised again by the power he still had over her after all these years. When she was a puppy, what an ignorant fool she'd been! He would play with her ears, paws, tail—what a fine friend! Only to learn it was all a ruse. Out of nowhere, among the frolicking, a poke and a yelping pinch right on the rump! Not a hint of playfulness anymore, but a stern expression behind the wire-framed glasses. "Good Girl," he praised. *Oh, those pesky annual shots.*

Passersby often stopped at the large bay window overlooking the street to admire Atlas, Doc's silver Weimaraner. Atlas spent business hours lounging on his plush, monogrammed bed in the window, his translucent velvet coat on full display. He wasn't the only one treated like royalty. No waiting room was more inviting. When you opened the front door, you were greeted with the lovely voice of Patty Paige singing the old, "How Much Is That Doggie in the Window?" The recording was motion-sensored, so Doc and Atlas heard this endearing tune dozens of times a day. They never tired of it. Rae especially adored the part when the puppy chimed in *"Woof, woof!'* There were dog and kitty beds next to each chair, a basket of toys, and a jar of treats on the counter.

It was after nine o'clock and long dark outside. The light in the waiting area had been turned off and the door locked. Doc was finishing up a busy day. Both his vet technician and his receptionist had recently resigned after nearly twenty years with him. The field of veterinary medicine had become oppressive, to say the least. They'd left when Doc was handed a paint brush and ordered by Chief Jerkins to paint the sign on his door. It had read *Doc's Place.* In front of a crowd of gawkers and a gun-toting officer, he'd added a brush stroke to the letter "C" to convert it to a "G", so that the door read *Dog's Place. Dog* had become the number two dirty word on the street, second only to *canine.* The two loyal employees had fled in tears. Without his staff, he had his hands full handling all aspects of his practice, which had shrunk by about thirty percent in the last month. Some dogs had moved out of Daffy County; others were keeping a low profile.

"Come, Atlas. I need your help," he called. Atlas jumped from his bed in the window and galloped through the swinging door to the back office. Doc grabbed the broom from the utility closet and swept the floor. He hung his white doctor's coat on a closet hook and buttoned his winter jacket, car keys in hand.

Suddenly, a tremendous crash came from the front room. He nearly fell backward. Atlas immediately obeyed Doc's cue to remain quiet. It was an identifiable sound though Doc had never heard it before, the way you know it's a bear without ever before having heard a live growl.

He regained steadiness when he heard a second crash just as jarring as the first. It left him with no doubt: He was under attack. He waved Atlas into the closet with him and turned off the lights. He gripped Atlas at the nape and held his breath.

Someone was pounding on the front door, which flew open. Patty Paige's sweet voice floated out, singing "How Much Is That Doggie In The Window?"

"*Woof, woof,*" barked the puppy. The innocence of the music, a child's carefree melody, had suddenly become eerily out of place. Heavy footsteps assaulted Patty and her little pup and barged through the swinging door into the back office, a mere arm's length away. Doc remained crouched in a tight ball, Atlas' silver head buried in his jacket—sitting ducks at the mercy of the intruders. There were sounds of opening cabinets, spilling paper, tossing books. Laughter and whoops came from a deep voice and from another only halfway to manhood. Within moments, the footsteps rumbled back into the waiting room and out the front door.

Then, utter silence. Neither of them moved. After a few tense moments, Doc pulled himself up and cracked open the closet door. The clock ticked, and the oil burner hissed gently. He didn't dare turn on the light, but he could see through the darkness that he had been ransacked. Papers and books cluttered the floor. His financial records were scattered, his appointment book gone.

As much as he dreaded it, he inched the swinging door open. A gust of frigid air engulfed him, and he knew his instincts had been right. The large bay window had been shattered. A few sharp daggers of glass remained intact, jutting out at violent angles. Atlas' fancy bed sparkled in a pool of broken glass reflecting off the street light. Silicate shards and debris blanketed the floor and covered the beds and chairs.

Doc let out a single cry, keys still clutched in his fist. He knelt on the shattered remains of twenty-five years of his career. Something trickled down his face, and he wondered if he'd been hit by a maverick shard. But when he wiped his cheek, it was not blood that he saw. It was tears.

He would be cleaning meticulously through the night. But first he swept only a small area in the center of the room and a path for Atlas. He turned on the music. It was a jazzy tune, one of Violet's favorites. He began to hum along in the aching, street-lit shadows. "Atlas," he asked, "do you want to dance?" The Weimaraner pranced toward him, his front paws nearly reaching Doc's chest. Doc held him so that Atlas was standing majestic and tall.

They danced. Doc lead the way, the two making slow, careful rotations the way he and his wife, Violet, had on her last good morning. By then, only a few wispy strands had been left of her hair, and darkness had circled her eyes. It had been five years, but it felt like yesterday. On the morning before hospice took over, it was this song they had danced to. Her arms had been limp in his, with Doc humming in her ear.

THE BAND OF ROGUE CITIZENS FANNED OUT, shouting and bellowing through the business sections of Blundertown and the surrounding villages. They carried out a wild spree leaving a sickening trail of destruction and glass behind them. They were a team of thugs emboldened by their numbers and by the night, when no one was present to defend their businesses—neither the pet stores nor the veterinarians, the groomers, the boarders. At each business the glass was left strewn on the sidewalks, the interiors ransacked and looted. The officer on duty sat idly by, chewing her gum in a marked car at the curb, watching. She was following instructions.

What a mess the streets were the next morning! The officer took a report from Doc straight away. He pulled out his note pad and began to write as Doc described the incident. But before he was finished telling his account of what happened, the officer ripped the top page from his pad and handed it to him.

"What's this?"

"A citation," the officer said matter-of-factly. "As the business owner of these premises, you're responsible for maintaining the public sidewalk in front here. You've got twenty-four hours to clean it up." He didn't look at Doc when he said it. Had he, he would have seen a crushed man behind the wire-framed lenses. And if he had looked more closely still, he would have seen a small flame of anger, stoked and raging, burning through the glass.

CHAPTER 8

Lifespan Of A Club

MY FAMILY WAS GOING OUT *on a frigid Sunday morning. Mother wore a black fur coat, fuzzy hat, and gloves. Daddy's fists made bulges in his coat pockets, and Jack wore oversized mittens. They were walking away from our house, snow all around them. Delicate white lines traced the barren trees.*

I wasn't with them. I was standing alone in the side yard, but there it was springtime. Everything was in full, vibrant color. Pink-white blossoms burst from our magnolia tree. Penny rested on the lawn, a sliver of sunshine emanating through each shoot, and the air was warm and fragrant. I felt Iggy wiggle in my arms, and I realized she had become a real iguana! She leaped from me and skittered among the tulips— bold purple, red, and yellow— twitching and nibbling the way real iguanas do. Penny joined her.

At the edge of the lawn, a dividing line separated me from my family, still walking away in wool and fur. "Hey! Mommy!" I called out. No one heard me. "Hey! Guys!" I shouted louder. My father smiled at me, mildly curious that I wasn't with them. My brother waved his giant mitten, his silver braces flashing. Mother seemed to look right through me. "Look! It's springtime over here! Come over here!"

My father scooped up some snow with his bare hands. Brr. Then he hurled something across the invisible line to me. A snow-ball landed at my feet. I picked it up and wiped away the layers. In my hand was a large seed, a compact bundle of potential the size of a walnut. Penelope dug a small hole and I planted the seed there, covering it with a blanket of dirt as my family receded into the distance.

RAELYN WAS WELL ACQUAINTED with the United Front. It was the unified position her folks took on parenting matters, whether they actually agreed or not. A United Front made for good parents with well-adjusted, capable children who would one day be good parents with United Fronts themselves. Disagreements between them happened behind closed doors; never let your children see the crack in the United Front, or they'll dive in for the kill like sharks—hungrily, no holds barred. Children were intuitively good at this, and Rae was no exception. It's just that she rarely got the chance. The Devine Front was impenetrable, especially when Jack wasn't around to poke holes in it.

On the evening after Doc Goodman's frightful night, her mother was at work and Raelyn tested the waters over dinner. "Dad, who were those people who did those things?"

"What things?"

She looked at the newspaper squarely in front of him. The headline read *Corrupt Canine Businesses Pay Price,* with a photograph beneath it of a smashed store window. "The things right in front of you. You know, Doc Goodman."

"Oh, those things."

"Yeah, *those* things."

"Well, no one knows."

"*Some*one knows. The people who did it know. The cops must know."

"Well, not exactly. The police aren't involved."

"Didn't anyone get arrested?"

"Not the folks who did it."

"But people get arrested all the time for a whole lot less." She was referring to her brother, of course, and the increasing number of detainments.

Her father squirmed in his chair. Truth was, Chief Jerkins had ordered the police to sit out the events the previous night, and he knew it: alas, those emergency powers. "Raelyn, sometimes I don't like what I see, either," he began. "Some things—there's not a lot we can do about."

"But there must be *something* we can do." Pause. "Dad." She waved an invisible screen in front of his face and smiled. "*Hellooooo.*"

"Well, you know how your mother feels about all of this."

Aha! There it was: a crack. She might get somewhere. It was the first time she could recall her father framing anything that way, singling out *your mother* instead of the all-inclusive, un-touchable *We*. She sat higher in her chair. "Yeah. You don't have to like it, but it's the law. Every battle is not yours to fight."

He cleared his throat. "She's right, you know. I pretty much agree with her on some of this." But his voice wavered.

"Well, I don't. And I'm going to do something." It sounded defiant. Never mind that she had no idea what she was talking about; it was merely a test for him to pass.

"Like what?" He'd passed. His voice was curious and calm.

"Like. . .I don't know."

Penelope cocked her head and looked up at her. *What do you mean, you don't know?*

Rae reached down and massaged her velvety ears. How could she? How could she use Penelope as a cheap ploy to get a reac-tion from Dad? Of course she meant it. She really *would* do something. Penelope, don't you worry.

Another pause. "What about your friends? What do they think?"

This was an unexpected question—her father asking about sixth-graders' views on such a serious adult topic. She didn't know the answer. She was just as silent among her peers as the grownups were about the Canine Problem (as it came to be known). Troubling images jumped out at her: the math problems and strange civics lessons, armies of walking armbands in the halls, the Student-of-the-Month Award to the OK! Club presi-dent, Ginnie Harper. A seventh-grader had been suspended when his parents were accused of Ration Fraud to buy extra dog food.

He was instantly un-friended *en masse.* The Canine Problem was alive and well at school.

She told her father all of these things. Instead of cutting her off ("that's enough, Raelyn"), he sat and listened even after she stopped speaking. Then he scratched behind his ear and took a bite from his plate. Then another. On the third, he finally spoke. "So how do you know if others feel the same way you do?"

"Gee, I can't go around school interviewing people." She made a microphone with her fist. "Are you against smashing windows?" Penny cocked her head at the question. "Is the ration too small?" Her head tilted opposite, awaiting answers.

"I suppose not." Yet another delay. "Something to think about, anyway."

Later that evening, Raelyn wrestled with his words. She lay in her sleeping bag on the living room floor with Penny on the outside. It was their ritual Friday-night sleepover. What had her father meant? He was telling *her* to think. She stroked Penny's long, soothing back, the fur thick and deep between her fingers. She and her father seemed to share an unspoken understanding. There must be others like her with the will to do something. But it wouldn't be him; he was not the man-of-action type. Penelope transcended into quiet, rhythmic snoring, probably dreaming of happier times. Raelyn would be dreaming soon, too, after watching her stunning Glitterfest. It seemed that her next chapter was written. The gentle, go-ahead wink from her father—his blessing—was all she had needed.

The following Monday at school, colors of everything appeared a shade brighter. Hidden good luck charms nestled in clandestine places. As she zigzagged through the crowds, she noticed how many students were *not* wearing armbands rather than how many were. She was immersed in a sea of potential allies, *confidantes*, people with whom she could only communicate by code and signal. It was like having the lead role in a spy movie. *Calling all sane people, wink, wink.*

She had never made an appointment with Guidance before, but she knew who Mr. Esperanza was. Every sixth-grade girl did, and many (she wasn't telling) had a crush on him. He had a scrubbed-clean appearance and didn't look much older than the boys at Jackson's place. His office smelled of manly cologne. He offered her a Tootsie Roll. As soon as she bit off a chunk, she wished she hadn't. Talking wasn't easy while eating a Tootsie Roll, and her teeth were coated with dark, gooey chocolate. With her mouth closed, all the syllables that eked through sounded more or less the same.

"So, Raelyn, are you in any sports?"

"Yuh."

"Which ones?"

"Sshuf-vull" (*translation: softball; not true until spring*).

"How do you like it?"

"Guhd" (*didn't know yet*).

"What's your favorite class?"

"Sshunce" (*translation: science*).

"Really. Why science?"

"Uh dunnuh" (*she liked the logic and proof, the method to*

the madness).

By the time he asked the real question, her Tootsie Roll was gone. "So, Raelyn, what brings you here?"

"I want to form a new club." It sounded surprisingly self-assured. A poster on his wall showed a winding path leading toward a bright blue castle in the clouds: *The Impossible Dream. . .isn't.*

Mr. Esperanza leaned toward her with hands in prayer position, chin resting on the fingertips. "Oh? About what?"

The sun filtered through the blinds and created stripes on her. The slightest wrong move made her squint, and she fidgeted for the perfect position. She looked again at the grand fortress on the wall. Jackson's fourth clue materialized as she stared at the poster:

> *Somewhere in school*
> *You'll find a life rule:*
> *A vision unattainable, absurd*
> *Summed up in a four-letter word.*

She followed the winding path into the clouds, traced the broad loops of the calligraphy. *The Impossible Dream. . . .*

"Isn't," she murmured.

"What's that?" Mr. E's forehead wrinkled.

She smiled, victorious. "Four letters. The impossible dream. It's '*Isn't*', isn't it?"

"It is!" Mr. Esperanza broke into a wide, perfect grin.

"Wait." She was confused, "It's '*is*'?"

"Exactly!"

"Isn't it '*isn't*'?"

"Yes. It's '*isn't*'."

Finally, she was getting somewhere. She now had G, E, I, __,
__, __.

"The impossible dream *isn't* impossible," he explained. "Nothing is impossible, so anything is possible!" He flung his arms wide. "So, about your club."

IEG, GIE, EGI.

"Raelyn?"

She snapped out of her thoughts. "Oh, right. Something about. . .something important to kids, like. . ." Mr. E had returned to quasi-prayer posture and was listening intently. "Their pets, I don't know." There. She'd said it, sort of.

"Ah!" His hands opened again, like half of a clap, and his face lit up. "A pet-owners club! That's a terrific idea."

This was a promising reaction, but she remained guarded. "Yeah. Like cats. Fish, turtles." She tried to keep her voice the same. "Dogs."

Mr. E leaned forward again, his expression more serious. "Do you know how a school club is formed?" She did not. "By an idea. It just takes an idea!" His voice was whispery and excited. "And if others share that idea, and you have the principal's permission, you have a club."

The Pet Lover's Club was thus born. Rae made posters announcing the first meeting, to be held the following Wednesday after school. Angelica helped her post them with tape from the main office. When she and Mr. E (the club advisor) met again before the meeting, she confided in him. What had motivated her was the Canine Problem. If other students were interested, who knew? Perhaps they could build a private park where dogs could play, or bake doggie treats for the upcoming holidays. Or hold a fundraiser to help business owners like Doc Goodman fix their windows. As she rattled off ideas, she felt a fledgling optimism and maturity she had never recognized before. She had taken a definitive step from a child to a near teenager, the vibrant castle floating majestically in the clouds.

"See you at the club after school," she said to Angie, both in coordinated head bands, miniskirts, and wool tights. They were parting ways at the intersection of Corridors B and C.

"Oh," Angie called, "I can't." A river of students had already seeped into the space between them. "My mom's coming home today!" Rae was swept away by the current.

Really? Her best friend had just told her *now?* She stomped into the locker room and switched into sneakers, the laces cutting into her fingers. Angie's mother was coming home from somewhere all the time, it's what she did.

No, the reason was that Angie knew her too well and didn't support the club. Period. But to lie about it! She shouldn't have been surprised; the Quinns had never been dog people. They had two cats. And Angie knew the club was all-inclusive. Raelyn threw her boots in the locker. She tossed the headband in the garbage. You know what, Angie? So long, it's been good to know you.

THE FINAL BELL BUZZED. She walked briskly down the hall toward Room 310 and was put at ease by the sight of Mr. Esperanza. Her notebook read Pet Lover's Club—Agenda and had the date. She watched the blur of adolescence whiz by. Eventually, a seventh-grade girl entered the room, followed by another named Nori. Several more students came—three boys (one named Dawson) and a girl, then her friends Megan and Cierra and two eighth-graders. And one of them was Gil Richmond. When he saw her, he stopped in the doorway and turned to leave. Then he faced the room again, sauntered in, and slouched into a desk in the very back of the classroom. His lips made a sarcastic move directly at her.

Rae's legs weakened, and a cave formed in her belly. She was mortified—exactly what he would want. Surely, he thought her a snob, never answering. But he had it all wrong. She was just clumsily inert due to circumstances beyond her control. What was a girl to do? One thing was clear right now: To make it through the meeting, she had to convince herself he wasn't there. She hid behind her curtain of black curls.

On the other hand, perhaps he was here for Prince. It was the Pet Lover's Club, after all.

"Where's Angie?" Cierra asked. Raelyn rolled her eyes but said nothing.

She counted eleven people in the room, including herself and the advisor. This was more than enough for an official club. She breathed a bit more easily. But even with 4-H under her belt and Megan, Cierra, and Mr. E sitting near her, public speaking was nerve-wracking—especially when it really mattered and there was someone in the audience who hated you. She dropped her pencil. She dropped her notebook. Then everyone introduced themselves and shared the names and types of their pets. The tally was five cats, eight dogs, two tanks of fish, one rabbit, and a snake named Armon. The group brainstormed, and there were some peculiar ideas. The skinny snake boy suggested a fundraiser where people paid for hugs from Armon's three foot, muscular body. Mr. E diplomatically nixed the idea.

When Rae shared her ideas about dogs, the room grew silent.

". . .Could we get in trouble for that?" Megan cautioned.

"It's not illegal," Rae assured her. Mr. E nodded in agreement. "It's just. . ." she searched for the word.

"Controversial?" he suggested.

Yes, that. A student whose cat was named Tickles stood up and silently left the room. No goodbyes, nothing. Raelyn turned to her advisor, whose head was lowered as if to say, "Don't mind her. Carry on."

Cierra commented, "I'd have to ask my mom first," and several others nodded in agreement.

Rae found herself in defense mode. "We're not making any big statement. We'd just be helping our own pets and other dogs."

A loud, clear voice turned everyone's attention to Nori. "I think we should do it. I think what's been happening is awful. My family—we love our Bella."

"Canine lover!" a blonde boy heckled. A few chuckles followed from scattered places in the room.

"Yeah, I am," Nori retorted, "and proud of it!" Way to go, Nori, but Rae was getting extremely nervous.

"*Ooh*," an eighth-grade girl teased, provoking smirks and a few more cackles.

By then, Mr. Esperanza was standing with his hands in blocking position. "Let's be open-minded. Folks have differing opinions."

"Right, and I'm a Canine Hater!" the heckler boy shouted. Things went quickly out of control. Several loud boos joined the mix, and Rae's insides were scrambled. Mr. E tactfully escorted the heckler to the door. This was a voluntary club with rules of civility, he explained. The meeting tried to get back on track when Snake Boy jumped up, chanting, "Armon! Armon!" Gil was laughing in the back, his huge sneakers sprawled way out in front of him. There were three students in the room who had remained silent, and he was one of them. All three had dogs, and all were wimps in her opinion. Thanks a lot, guys.

The meeting was adjourned and a second one scheduled for a week later, when the membership would vote on the activities.

RAE WAS GUARDEDLY OPTIMISTIC about the second meeting. In spite of the drama, a fair number had expressed interest. Maybe they'd bring their friends this time. That was how these things worked, by word of mouth. And there were always Cierra and Megan. Who needed Angelica anyway? She waited in Room 310 with Mr. Esperanza. The chatter in the hall hit its peak and began to thin. Gil Richmond entered and sat in the same distant seat he had the week before. The same hollow formed in her gut. Occasional footsteps approached and faded.

It was soon two-thirty. Fifteen minutes had passed. She wondered where Cierra was; she'd sounded like she was coming. So did a few newcomers, Josh and Kate. Come to think of it, though, none of them had looked her in the eye. Nori had approached earlier that day. "My parents told me to stay out of it. I'm sorry." Even Snake Boy hadn't shown. At 2:35, it was clear that no one else was coming. Mr. Esperanza cleared his throat and looked at her.

"Should I start?" she asked quietly.

He made an effort to smile. "Raelyn, there have to be a minimum of four members for a school club to hold a meeting. It's in the by-laws."

"Oh." He had told her that, she remembered. She glanced across the long room to Gil, smug in the back row, mocking her. It was impossible to pretend he wasn't there when no one else was. She took her time gathering her things, waiting for him to leave first.

Mr. E placed his hand on her shoulder. "You know how many resumes I sent out before I got this job?" he asked her after Gil was gone. She had no clue how many. She'd be a fool to guess. "Twenty-nine," he went on. "But it was worth it. Because this is the best job I could ever ask for." He latched his bag. "Kids like you inspire me more than you can know. The *maturity*." He tossed his coat over the crook of his arm, an awesome smile on his face. "And the—the *fresh intelligence* of you kids at your age, that's what sets you middle-schoolers apart." She blushed.

As they approached the door, he smiled again. "Did you know that Walt Disney was fired from a newspaper job because he lacked imagination and good ideas?" She did not know that! "Disney. My point is, don't give up."

"Mr. Esperanza." The school principal was at the door. She was wearing an orange armband.

"Yes?"

"I'd like a word with you in my office."

Mr. E gave Raelyn a wary smile and followed his boss down the hall.

Alone on the late bus home, she didn't know what bothered her more: being let down by friends and classmates (especially Angelica), the puncture to her pride, Gil Richmond going out of his way to torment her. And, hello—when did this whole thing become about her; wasn't it supposed to be about poor little Penelope? Who was the big ego head now? Besides, she had no business judging the other students. She hadn't even told her own parents about the Pet Lovers Club. She was the biggest coward of all, no different from her own folks. What goes around comes around.

She held her chin high in school and acted as if none of it had ever happened. She avoided Angie as much as possible. And when she couldn't, she gave her a cool shoulder. After all, it was arguably her fault. Had she been a true friend and simply shown up, others would have too; she had that effect. They would have more than met the quota. But never mind. What a joke it had been, so easy to have forgotten.

That is, until she stopped by Mr. Esperanza's office one day soon afterward and saw a new guidance counselor sitting at his desk.

Mr. E had been transferred to the elementary school where he was confined to six- and seven-year-olds. He had been demoted. The fairy tale castle, a silly mirage, had vanished from the sky.

CHAPTER 9

A New And Improved Game Of Hide-And-Seek

I WAS PLAYING HIDE-AND-SEEK *with Jack and Penelope at the park. In real life, he made sure I was always partnered up. I would hide with Penelope and he'd find us, or Penny and I would find him.*

Well, in my dream, they were hiding together and I was the lone seeker. I covered my eyes with my hands and buried my face on the picnic table, as always—two levels of protection from cheating—and counted to fifteen. "Ready or not, here I come!" I opened my eyes. I turned full circle for a panoramic view. The park was bordered by Old Wood trees all around. I circled again, but nothing gave me a hunch or a direction. The swing set was empty, the baseball diamond abandoned. In the distance was the lonely gazebo. I scoured the trees for a hint of his red shirt, but there was nothing. No slight movement, no small yelp from Pene-

lope. Not a soul.

"Jack!" I cried. I called more desperately, "Jack! Penny!"
But the park was empty. I had just lost them both.

Hide-and-seek had ceased to be a game.

Well, this was most unusual. Her doctor paying a visit? At her home, no less, and after dark? If memory served, the church bells had rung a string of times. The family had gone upstairs, and all the lights in the house were out. Penelope was well into the night shift when the doorbell rang. What a fright! Any number of dangerous critters could have been there, but fortunately, it was her beloved Doc. The strangeness of things was becoming routine, but she was unsettled by it. Her doctor had visited a few times before with a slew of others in the midday sun, with enticing aromas curlicuing from the barbecue. But not like this. There was no doubt in her mind: This visit was about her.

She was lying in the corner of the kitchen, keeping an eye on things. Doc looked different without his white coat, but he smelled the same. He sat in his bulky jacket next to Alpha and father in their scented slippers and bathrobes, rare attire for company. No coffee, tea, or a morsel to eat, and all three with stern, tired faces. Doc removed his glasses and rubbed his eyes. Her ears pricked when he spoke. Then Alpha asked him a question.

ALPHA: *But why? When?*
DOC: *The end of the week. It's too dangerous to continue.*

The father cleared his throat, but it was Alpha who spoke again.

ALPHA: *The vandalism, it's inexcusable. But, to close your practice? I mean, aren't you giving a handful of thugs exactly what they want?*
FATHER: *(arm across the back of Alpha's chair). Honey, I'm sure it feels more personal to Ken.*

A small sound came from the hallway. Penny glanced through the open door and saw Raelyn tiptoeing from the top of the stairs in the dark.

DOC: *It's more than just the damage and the broken glass. It's the citation, the exorbitant fines I'm expected to pay for the street. (Looks down at hands). Today I received notice that my license is suspended. So-called "office failure." When they came to inspect, all of my records were in tatters.*

Rae was now at the bottom of the stairs in her airy nightgown. *Tsk, tsk, the child has been sneaking candy up to her room again,* Penelope's nostrils flared knowingly. The kitchen light beamed a bright triangle into the hall. Raelyn was standing just outside of it and then did something rather curious. She crouched on all fours and began to crawl toward them. *How rather interesting! She wants to get the low-down about this important visit, too,* Penny surmised.

DOC: *But I didn't come here at this late hour to talk about me. I came about* Penelope.

Bingo! It most assuredly was about her! She couldn't resist an "I told you so" wag. She wasn't boasting, mind you, but she did want Raelyn to know that *she* was the subject of this vital meeting. But her sister didn't seem to notice. She was having trouble with four-legged travel. Her nightgown was caught under her knees and the fabric had pulled her to a halt. She released the gown and proceeded to move forward, only to get caught up in the same way. She had quite a distance to cover. As she struggled, her hair plopped in front of her face, and she looked like a mop *(but no worries; she wasn't, thank goodness)*. She pushed the mop of hair away and continued in this clumsy fashion toward the kitchen door. She certainly was no agile four-legged like herself.

Raelyn was then centered in the light. Doc would see her if he looked her way, but he gave no sign. She gave up crawling. Penny watched as she stretched both arms in front of her and propelled the rest of her body forward, sliding across the polished floor—a more graceful means of travel for her. Finally, she reached the kitchen door and huddled behind it. Only then did she seem to notice Penelope in the corner. She pressed a finger to her lips. How endearing, Penny mused, as if she hadn't been keeping Rae's cover since the top of the stairs. She signaled twice by tail and turned back to the adults.

FATHER: *Go on.*

DOC: *When are you scheduled to register* Penelope?

Again! Penny's ears twitched.

ALPHA: *Tomorrow afternoon, why?*

DOC: *Once she is registered, she's no longer safe. You know that, right?*

ALPHA: *But we have to register her. It's the law. We could be arrested.*

DOC: *There's an alternative.*

ALPHA: *(hint of impatience) What do you mean?*

DOC: *(to father) Vigil, I've known you for thirty years. I've treated* Penelope *since she was a tiny puppy. (Yet again!) I trust I have your confidences?*

FATHER: *(takes her doctor's hand, smiles) Kenny, I couldn't have earned my Eagle badge without you—all those crazy nautical knots. We attended each other's wedding. (Smile disappears) Violet's funeral. You can count on us.*

DOC: *(eyes close, then open) If you register her, I can't help you. But if you don't, I'll do my best to keep her safe.*

ALPHA: *How?*

DOC: *I'll hide her. I can accommodate up to fifteen dogs in my cellar. Penelope can be one of them. Before the rations, I hoarded food for weeks. I can't make any promises, but I'll do my best until this whole mess blows over.*

ALPHA: *(gasping) Why, Doc! (throws head back, nose facing*

*ceiling, gives little laugh). You can't be serious? Hide our
dog?*

FATHER: *(squeezing the back of Alpha's chair) What Joan
means is—look, Ken, it's a lot to process. It's very generous of you. Can we get back to you?*

DOC: *Certainly. But I can only hold her spot until six tomorrow. (Stands) I'll be in my office, closing files. There
are only a few spaces left, I'm afraid. Good night to you
both, and Happy Holidays.*

Instead of leaving, he came *directly over to her!* He petted gently
up and down her crest and withers and looked her in the eye.
"Good night, Penelope." He kissed her on the nose. Then he gave
her whole body a tremendous hug and patted her mightily on the
chest. She couldn't stop licking her doctor, she loved him so!

The father patted Doc's back just as heartily at the door, and
Doc left. Raelyn quietly skittered up the stairs. The parents retreated upstairs too, and the door squeaked shut, lights off.
Penny curled up at the foot of the steps, satiated by all the attention but quite nervous just the same.

Moments later, Raelyn's bedroom door opened, and Penelope
noticed a faint whiff of goose down. Rae tiptoed downstairs
again, this time dragging an open sleeping bag and pillow. "Hi,
My Lady," she whispered. She plopped the sleeping bag down
and leaned over her, resting her cheek against her fluffy neck.
"How about a sleepover? It's not Friday, but so what?" She
slipped feet-first into the bag and shared the pillow with Penny.

They snuggled as they always did and kissed each other good night. But Raelyn squeezed her extra tightly tonight. "I love you." Penny's eyelids closed. She gave a long, exhausted sigh, and her breaths deepened.

Rae closed her eyes, too, and waited for her Glitter. The colors entered with cautious energy. The faded pinks twinkled. The grays rotated in slow, hesitant motion. *Come on, you can do better than this.* She watched the pastels swirl like sleepy, midnight dancers. Deep teal ripples disappeared into a murky sea. *All's right with the world,* she tried assuring herself. Tomorrow would be here all too soon. It was time for a promising dream, an inspirational, somnolent tale. Time for a miracle.

AT BREAKFAST, RAE PLEADED with her parents not to register Penelope, without letting on that she'd overheard everything the night before. Penny was trapped in her desperate embrace.

"Raelyn, it's the *law*," her father said, taking the phrase right out of Mom's playbook. There was no hint of recognition of his daughter's confidences only two weeks before.

"But *why*? What's the *point* of it?"

"That's not our concern, love," her mother said.

Rae wanted to know, "What's the worst thing that could happen if we didn't?"

Her mother wasn't having any of it. "Frankly, I don't want to know. We've been through all this. She's a dog. A canine. . .and *please* lower your voice." Her shoes click-clacked all over the kitchen as she poured more coffee, rinsed dishes, took a gulp, wiped the counter. Dad's nose was in the morning paper as usual.

Rae blinked at both of them, but they were all a blur. *Mars to parents*, she messaged via brainwaves across the kitchen. But there was no one on the receiving end. It was her last, futile attempt. Sometimes it truly sucked being a kid. It sucked even more without a brother or a best friend.

ON REGISTRATION DAY, *What a long line!* Penelope waited with Alpha and Raelyn among all the other families. Who knew there were so many of us, she marveled. The mood was irritable, the air thick with anxiety and sweat. When it was their turn, the woman at the desk stamped forms and rattled off a series of questions without looking up: "Date of last rabies shot? Ever bite anyone? Growl?" She stamped the top of the form. "Next," she called. They moved to the next station. "One hundred dollars," the man bellowed. Items were exchanged. At the third station, Penelope watched a beagle and his family in front of them. The worker removed the beagle's collar and tossed it in a box.

"Hey!" barked the beagle. *"That's my collar! Give that back!"* The worker swatted the beagle on the nose. *"Hey! That hurt! What'y'do that for?"* The worker hit him again. *"Ouch!"* the beagle cried, and was met with a third painful smack on his nose. This time, the beagle stayed quiet. The worker fit him snugly with a new collar that had numbers across it. The line moved on.

A distant memory percolated of a mop head raining down on her muzzle. Penelope would do now what she learned to do then:

She would be a very, very good girl. When it was her turn, she sat like the perfect lady that she was. The worker removed her designer necklace.

Raelyn was hysterical. "I *made* that collar for her! It was a birthday present!"

My goodness, Alpha, will you do something here? But all she did was put an arm around her daughter and say, "Sweetie, hush." Penny's jewelry, the elaborately woven pink-and-gold pattern with the silver name tag, was tossed in the garbage. A plastic County-issued collar was tightened around Penny's neck. It was the same as the beagle's but with different numbers. "It must wear its number at all times," the worker ordered. Alpha handed the worker a bag with Penelope's belongings, including her favorite blanket, a few toys, toiletries, and a special note from Raelyn. The worker tossed the bag onto the heap behind him.

FOR WEEKS, DOC GOODMAN'S WARNING reverberated in Raelyn's head. She approached each day expecting the other shoe to drop, or the sky to fall. But winter break came and went. The New Year rang in without incident. School had resumed, and Penelope was still safe. Perhaps it had been all hype. Perhaps the worst was over.

Then a notice came through the squeaky mail slot at 12 Hucklepuddy Road. Penelope approached it with suspicion. It smelled identical to the first one that afternoon long ago—a metallic, dirty fragrance, quite offensive to a sniffing connoisseur like herself. And they were the same color. Contrary to popular belief, dogs see more than black-and-white. The two pieces of mail were the same shade, depth, hue, and tint. It was no coincidence, of this she was certain. *Something rotten this way comes.*

She huddled with it under the desk and waited for Raelynn. When she finally arrived, Penelope greeted her with drooped ears and the notice in her jaw. Raelyn dropped her backpack. She pulled off her gloves and examined the mauled paper in silence. She sank to her knees. Penny kissed her on the face and the glasses, but there was no T-R-E-A-T today. Suddenly, Rae grabbed the numbered collar and leash. "Penny, we're going to take a very long, W-A-L—" she stopped.

She put the leash back down. "The curfew, sorry." Penny's tail dropped, and her flews sagged into a frown. She relegated herself to the moping place under the desk and gazed into the floor. *All is well,* she told herself as she began licking her paws. *All is well.* Lick, lick, lick, lick.

Rae hopped on her bike. Round-Up Day was January 25, the notice said. That was *tomorrow*. Registered dogs would be brought to Daffy County's canine compound, a newly constructed, temporary housing and training facility on the outskirts of Blundertown. The Blundertown Compound was "necessary to restore safety and cleanliness to our communities; visiting hours to be posted in the immediate future." In spite of her parents, she would accept Doc Goodman's offer to hide Penelope. She pedaled in the cold to Chestnut Street, but she was too late. A sign on his office door read *Closed Until Further Notice*. The large bay window had been replaced, but the waiting room inside was empty. Gone were the fluffy beds, the "Good Dog" treats on the counter, the litter box. Gone were the adorable posters of puppies and the bulletin board stuck with thank-you cards. For some reason she tried the door. To her surprise, it opened. The second door, however, was locked. A small, folded piece of paper was wedged there. . .with her name on it.

She stuffed it into her pocket, gave a fleeting look around, and rode off, dodging patches of black ice and snow on the sidewalks. She'd gotten her first bike for her sixth birthday and instantly fallen in love with it. When winter came, she refused to stop riding, snow or not. She'd been a year-round cyclist ever since. There was nothing like the freedom of her bike, but now it had become Penelope's lifeline. After a few blocks, she stopped. A K9 patrol car slowed to a crawl nearby, and she hid against a tree until it passed. She unfolded the note. It read simply, *376 Elmheart Ave.* Doc's residence, she guessed, wondering why he would address it to her. She was certain he lived quite nearby. She had delivered gifts with her parents over the years and attended his wife's memorial. She had a decent sense of direction.

Eventually, she recognized the street and the hand-painted ferns on the mailbox. The shades were drawn. She clambored up the porch steps and rang the bell. A frilly basket of plastic violets still hung there, surely another remnant of the wife from years ago. It dawned on her how sad Doc sometimes looked even when he smiled. The window shade parted slightly, and he signaled her to go around to the back.

In the rear mudroom, he looked ten years older than he had

the last time she saw him. His eyes were dull, and the lines around his mouth sagged. He'd been expecting her. He explained that he'd seen her that late night from the kitchen while talking to her parents. She was shocked, but mildly impressed: So he'd known all along that she'd known all along! He offered her tea with honey.

"But how did you know I'd get the note?"

"I knew you'd try to find me. I know how much you love Penelope." He looked down at his stockinged feet. "Unfortunately, Raelyn, I can't help you now." His cellar was way over capacity. He had squeezed in one more dog, then another, then another, until he had doubled his intended population. They were under nearly sardine conditions as it was, and their food allotment was barely enough to sustain them. "If there's any other way I can help you, I will. Just knock twice on the back door." He saw her out and his eyes became watery. "Again, I'm very sorry."

Doc Goodman was not the only risk taker with a big heart in Blundertown. You'd never have guessed which ones they were because they were excellent secret-keepers, too. The Hagans had converted their attic into a clandestine Doggie Dormer suitable for twenty. Twenty beds, twenty water bowls, food bowls, chew toys, and muzzles. Muzzles, because have you ever tried keeping twenty dogs quiet all day and night for months? Mr. Hagan dug a hole in the back yard at four o'clock each morning to dispose of the dog doo and tracked each one with a mini snowman, furtive glances in all directions. Nineteen-year-old Veronica was hiding six pooches and her own Rocky in her walk-in closet. There were false walls and hidden stair cases in homes sprinkled throughout Daffy County.

There is a commanding knock on Doc's door. He peeks through the window shade in his bathrobe. It's Officer Osbourne and his partner, whom he doesn't know. They have seen his car; they know he's home. Sweat immediately percolates from his brow, and his heart quickens. As he opens the door, he prays that all his careful planning and carpentry will pay off.

"May I help you?" he asks in a steady voice.

"Good evening, Doc." Officer Osbourne tries to glimpse past him into the interior of the house. "Mind if we look around?"

"Of *course* I mind," Doc says, "unless you have a search warrant."

Unfortunately, they do. He swallows hard and lets them in, fingers crossed.

The partner makes his way upstairs. He peeks under the beds, behind hanging clothes in the closets. Doc follows Officer Oz around the living room, dining room, and kitchen as the chubby officer snoops and inspects.

"You live alone?" Officer Oz asks.

"I do." Doc's cell phone is playing music to drown out any noise from the basement.

"Any pets?

"If you mean dogs, no," he lies.

"Of course not, because that would be a crime, wouldn't it,

Doc?"

"But of course."

They're in the back hallway. It's dark because Doc unscrewed the light bulbs earlier in the week. The two men are dark, sepia figures standing at the basement door. Officer Oz turns the knob. It's locked. It's getting much harder for Doc to swallow. Saliva pools in his mouth, and his urge to spit becomes overwhelming. He has built additional walls and a second door at the bottom of the stairs, but he hopes the officer won't make it that far.

"Open the door."

He does as instructed. He cranks the music up to high volume—Mozart's Symphony 41. It's pitch dark, and Doc explains that the light is burned out in the stairwell, too. The officer fumbles for his flashlight, turns it on, and proceeds a few steps down the rickety staircase. He reaches along the wall, but there is no railing. Suddenly, the step he is on wobbles underfoot and he reaches behind him, making a dive for the landing. He bangs his hand. His flashlight crashes down the steps. "Geezus Pete," he mumbles.

"Careful, Officer—I believe there are a couple loose steps somewhere about there," Doc says. The officer asks for a flashlight, but regrettably, Doc doesn't have one. Officer Oz engages in a series of blind foot-taps on each step before gingerly placing his full weight on it. It's a slow process and, as it turns out, not a very reliable one. About half way down, the step he is on partially gives way. He loses his balance, and his arms wind-mill about. He again twists and lunges backward, catching himself to a stop. "Geezus Pete!" he curses.

"Careful," Doc says.

Office Oz claws his way to the top and is now hugging the landing. "How the heck do you ever get down these frigging stairs?"

"I don't. I haven't been down there for over a decade."

"Well, why didn't you say so?"

"You didn't ask."

"I did. Not. *Know.* To ask," he says with foolish fits and starts.

"Nor did I know, Officer, that you were inviting yourself to an unexpected tour of my home on such a fine evening," Doc quips.

The officer wipes the sweat off his face with the rim of his cap. He pauses at the top of the stairs and looks down again into the cavernous stairwell, contemplating whether to make another go of it. When he puts his cap back on, a cobweb teases his nose. He swats at it, spooked, first with his right hand, then his left.

"Geezus Pete," he shouts. He backs himself into the hall, off kilter and out of breath. "Is there another door to the basement?"

Doc tells him about the outside cellar door as he locks this one. From the window, he watches Oz stumble across the icy yard in the dark. At one point, the officer's boots fly out in front of him and he falls on his padded ass. Doc enjoys the officer's useless attempts at the frozen metal door. It doesn't budge, and the padlock is rusted. The officer forgot to ask him for the key.

Oz's partner has descended from the second floor and is waiting for him on his return. "Did you check the basement?" he inquires.

"Yep. All clear, Joe." Officer Osbourne flashes a threatening glare at Doc to keep quiet to spare him his pride. Doc perfectly complies.

"Let's clear out of here, then," the partner orders. He tips his hat. "Doctor."

"Leaving so soon? Do, please, come again unannounced and uninvited at odd hours of the night with a friendly, good natured search warrant." From his voice, you'd think he is smiling, but he isn't. He dead-bolts the door behind them.

Some folks are not as fortunate as Doc Goodman and his thirty clandestine dogs. Some officers are not as incompetent as Oz and Partner. Sometimes the Seekers find the Hiders. On her way home from school, Raelyn watched in horror as two officers escorted a group of dogs from a house, yanking on the leads and shouting. The dogs trotted reluctantly with their heads down. One was a golden retriever puppy. They marched in single file up the ramp and into the K9 patrol car. The puppy was last, his oversized paws (which he'd never grow into) prancing forward, his tail bopping with naïve excitement.

WE WON'T TALK ABOUT the following morning except to say that Raelyn refused to come out of her bedroom. In the wee hours, she clutched Penelope at the side of her bed, nose to nose, eyes of onyx locked and piercing in the dark. It was a scent Penelope had never smelled before, the pungent odor of defeat.

"We're the Rae-and-Penny team. Don't ever forget that."

Always and forever, My Little Raelyn.

"I'll visit you. And I promise I'll somehow bring you home. *I promise!*"

To her parents, she promised she would never, ever speak to them again for as long as she lived—and she hoped that wouldn't be long.

For days, every moment was a painful reminder. She exited the bus at 12 Huckypuddle Road. She and Angelica still weren't speaking, and she had no idea what to wear anymore. Her key opened the door, but there were no greetings: no slobbery kisses; no joyful, excited face. At night she lay there with Iggy, staring up into the dark, fifth wall that would entrap her for many nights ahead. She was sealed in a tomb of her own design, determined to shut out the universe. Good-bye, ugly world, been good to know you. She closed her eyes and waited for her much needed, comforting Glitter. She searched the edges of the darkness, the places from which the colorful dust usually appeared. For a long while, there was nothing. Eventually, a small grouping wandered in, dull and uninspiring. Another pale cluster was equally disappointing. She scrunched her face for greater darkness, but the sightings were painfully slim that night. When she needed her Glitter most, it was barely to be found. Perhaps tomorrow night, she tried assuring herself, for she knew it still must be there somewhere. Iggy wiped her face dry.

She must have drifted, because she awoke. What had begun as a gentle bodily hint had now become an announcement of some urgency. There was no ignoring it or willing it away any longer: She had to use the bathroom. She tossed her blankets aside and opened her reclusive door. Without her glasses, a fuzzy light shone from below. She stood, curious, at the top of the staircase. She descended a few steps and rested her forehead between the spindles of the banister.

There was her mother, somewhat bleary, sitting on the sofa in her black-and-white flannel nightgown, her slippers propped on the low table. Her hair had fallen over the side of her face, and there was a box of tissues at her hip. Several crumpled tissues were strewn about. "Oh, my," she mumbled, "I remember that day. . . ." She had the open photo album across her lap and a fresh tissue between her fingers. There she goes, Rae thought, talking to herself again! She covered her mouth to keep from giggling.

Then out of nowhere, her mother blew like a bugle into the tissue: a bellowing *honk!* that would raise eyebrows even coming from a grown man. If only Jack were beside her cracking up too, enjoying the covert entertainment with her. Her mother crushed the tissue in her fist and hurled it into the air with the strength of a Superhero. It floated pathetically to the floor. She grabbed another from the box and turned the page. There were more mutterings as she cocked her head back, a tissue across her face. Another mighty throw, roar! She had more quirks than you could count, the kids had always agreed. But as Rae continued to watch the private comedy from her balcony seat, it dawned on her that this was not a comedy at all.

Her mother was crying.

She had only seen her cry a few times in real life. Funerals, of course. Jack, of course. And at the movies (not real life), her mother was a complete embarrassment, sobbing over scenes that barely drew a lump to Rae's throat. Some mothers were like that. But she had never before seen her sniffling and sobbing alone in the glow of the living room. She turned another page and flung another tissue. It fell like a dying butterfly. Her face fell limp in her fists.

Rae remained riveted to the tortured image of her mother, surrounded by what now seemed a spray of dead flowers plucked mercilessly from their roots. She was mimicking her, fists clutching the railing. For a brief moment, the two of them, together, shared their grief alone. Suddenly an enormous sniffle interrupted them, followed by a cascade of choking sounds from below.

She didn't know what to make of her mother this way, but one thing was certain: She didn't want to see any more of it. Should she go down to her, she wondered, and what would she do when she got there? She took one step, then several more. She reached the top of the stairs. As she was about to turn into her bedroom, she was visited again by the urgency that had forced her out of bed in the first place. She dashed down the hall to the bathroom.

Despite what she had seen, Rae vowed in the morning to continue to her grave without ever speaking to her parents again. For several days, everyone respected the strained spaces and the impenetrable wall of dark, moody tresses over her face. Gradually, there was a grunt here, a "thank you" there. But on Day Four, out popped a full sentence, complete with comma and question mark: "Mom, can you sign this permission slip for school?" Her Life Goal blown so soon. It was all downhill from here, she told herself.

"Of course, sweetie. What's it for?"

It was for a field trip to Rae's favorite science museum. In spite of herself, she told her mother all about it.

CHAPTER 10

Postcard From Penelope

FINALLY MET THE TOOTH FAIRY IN A DREAM. *It was after my fourth lost tooth, a proud, vacant window in my grand smile. But I was a bit vexed. "Why didn't you ever write back?" I* demanded.

"Um," she began. *I studied her beauty, the smooth ebony contours of her face, the sparkly jewels woven through her hair. But the blank stare told me she had no response.*

"Hey," *it dawned on me,* "you're not real, are you?"

"Busted," *she replied with a wry smile.*

I found myself laughing, curiously satisfied. It all made sense now.

> *Dear Family,*
> 　　*Thank you for your letter(s) and / or gift(s).*
> 　　*I am doing very well. I enjoy two excellent meals a day, plus treats. We are bathed and*

groomed regularly and spend much of the day
playing with other dogs in the yard. I've made a
lot of new friends here.

See you soon. Woof, woof!

From your dog

"Well, see there, Raelyn," her father said. "All that doom and gloom for nothing. She's fine! The County is treating them very well."

Her mother held the card, her eyes teary with humor. "Isn't that just the cutest thing?" Rae looked at her, inquiring. "That Daffy County actually sends out these little postcards. It's adorable!"

To Rae, it had felt for a month and a half as if she were suffocating in a prickly wool sweater two sizes too small, tugging and scratching and reminding. As she looked at her parents' reassuring faces and the printed card, the fabric transformed into silk, draping lightly over her shoulders in soothing layers. Penelope was alright, after all. And yes, she had received her letters and gifts and everything. No more of Dad's teasing, "Our Gloomy Rae of Sunshine." Things were looking up.

"Absolutely adorable!" her mother said again. "They've thought of everything."

(Indeed, they had.)

What's more, after all those years the time finally came: Angie invited her to an opera starring her mother. Her timing was odd; they were hardly friends anymore, let alone best friends. They'd been estranged ever since Angie sabotaged the club and dove into her new friendship with Ginnie Harper. The two of them walked armband-in-armband around school—how nauseating—with Cierra and Megan always a step behind them. Rae swapped seats on the bus and sat with a girl named Monique. She learned that there was absolutely nothing wrong with Monique.

The theater invitation was a lame peace offering—too little, too late. But let's face it: Rae had always wanted to see for herself "the magic of the opera."

The performance was several hours away. They had excellent seats in the third row. She wore one of her only dresses, boring navy blue with a white collar. Angelica's was a full-skirted rose taffeta with a wide bow in the back and a matching ribbon in her curled hair. How typical. Her father, suit and bow tie, was carrying a huge bundle of red roses on his lap. The lights went out, and hushes hushed the audience.

It was one of the longest, most boring experiences she had ever sat through. She knew opera was singing, of course, but not that it was nothing *but* singing. There was no story to follow, no dialogue, and even if there had been, it was all in Italian. The voices were annoyingly loud and frilly, as if racing up and down ladders. No sooner would a voice reach the top than it would trill its way down to the bottom again. Angie's mother was on stage often—first with one man, then another, back and forth, and they seemed upset much of the time.

She glanced at Angie out of the corner of her eye, at the perfect curve of her spine, in rapt attention like her father. Rae daydreamed through most of it. She focused on Jackson's clues thus far: G, E, I. Then there was the as-of-yet unsolved Clue # 3 and the most recent, entirely baffling Clue # 5:

> *Look overhead in Springtime*
> *For the Great Bear in the sky*
> *A tilt of your head*
> *(You should be in bed)*
> *Marks who-what-when-where-why.*

She'd gotten nowhere with these and, frankly, she was beginning to lose interest. The clues were too hard. Jack was too smart, and she wasn't, and so much had happened since the game's innocent beginnings. Still, his game was a welcome distraction from the pain of missing Penelope. As the musicalities carried on, she found herself pondering Clue # 3 for the hundredth time. *"A lady's fine porch display / for many years and a day / needs neither sunshine nor water / whether cold or much hotter / these blossoms are here to stay."*

What kind of blossoms don't need water or sun? Surprisingly, the answer jumped out at her. Fake ones, of course! The basket of purple flowers on Doc Goodman's porch— they'd been there forever, long before his wife died. Violet's violets, duh! The plastic bouquet had been there when Raelyn bicycled to his house way back when, only to learn she was too late. G,E,I, and now a V. She played with combinations, V,I,G,E; V,I,E,G; V,E,I,G. Disjointed images floated up and down the ladder, mingling with the clues and the operatic voices: *E.* . . her English homework due tomorrow. . . . her *Igloo* project made from sugar cubes. *G.* . . Dad's famous grape jelly pancakes. Jack's *Viola* bow that Penelope ate once. Penelope. . .the postcard and her parents' mega smiles: *See you soon, woof, woof!*

Her wanderings abruptly stopped. Did you miss that? What did it mean, *See you soon?* There was no mention in the postcard of a release date. There still were no visiting hours, yet six weeks had passed.

The theater went ice-cold. *The postcard was a sham!* The stage became a blur of color, and the voices scattered.

Suddenly, the place was hit by thunder. "Bravo! Bravo!" Angie was standing and shouting, her curls bouncing. The entire house was on its feet: *"Bravo!"* Then the endless curtain calls: dramatic curtsies, bows, and blinding color. Rae was lost in an eruption of deafening cheers, clapping, and whistling.

"So what did you think of my mom?" Angie asked, breathless.

"She was really good." After a pause, she asked, "Did she die?"

"Of *course* she dies! Why else would she sink to the floor like that in the end?" She grabbed Rae's arm, laughing. "Come on, Gigi. Let's go see her back stage!" She acted as if they'd never stopped being friends. As VIPs, they were escorted down steps and through a hall where the star, Gloria Quinn, met them. Mr. Quinn handed the roses to Angie, who in turn gave them to her mother. This must be the way they did it. *"Bravissimo, Mom!"*

Angie was beaming. Her mother was a fright close-up. She had an outrageous amount of make up on (particularly around the eyes), which made her look freakish.

Rae dreaded ever being asked to the opera again, but the very next weekend, she was: another skimpy olive branch from her former best friend. She'd have to work a little harder than that. Apparently, Angie was offering her another crack at the storyline, since she'd clearly missed it. Rae sought advice during a visit with Jack—not about the dubious friendship (no one seemed to notice), or the lack of visiting hours with Penelope (no awareness there either), but about *La Traviata*.

"I don't blame you. Yech!" her brother cackled.

"Opera isn't for everyone," Dad agreed. "You could always decline."

"I'll tell you what!" Mom had a great idea. "You can tell Angie that you have other plans—and it will be true." She raised her eyebrows with a mischievous smile. "You and I can go shopping that day. How's that?" Peck, peck, give the young one a worm.

"Thanks, Mom!" As clueless as her mother was, she came through when Rae needed her most.

Sometimes.

CHAPTER 11

Angelica's Secret

NOW I WILL TELL YOU ABOUT *my most terrifying dream. It was so frightening that it chased my Glitter away. I was six, and my brother and I were playing catch with a big red ball. The ball got past me, and I ran after it. "Stop!" he called, "let it go!" In front of me was a hole in the lawn I'd never seen before. The ball rolled right into it and was gone. "It's a Bottomless Pit!" he screamed. I knew what he meant. He had teased me about the Bottomless Pit my whole life: no end, ever. You never hit bottom, no matter how far you fall or for how long. I tried desperately to catch myself at the edge, but it was too late. I lost my balance and plunged feet-first into the void.*

I fell, like Alice in Wonderland down the rabbit hole. But unlike Alice, I would never tumble to a stop. My descent was fast and horrifying, and my stomach leaped out of my throat. I could have been traveling through a black hole in outer space, but I was plummeting into the endless bowels of the Earth.

Night after night for a time, this dark dream tortured me: the sheer panic at the precipice, the terror of the fall. I began to hunker down, anticipating the daunting drop and the hopeless recognition of no way out. I concentrated for the Glitter to come—to rescue me, protect me from my fate—clutching Iggy, eyes squeezed tight. But there was blackness, nothing more.

Over time, the nightmare became an essential part of my bedtime routine: pajamas, brush teeth, kiss family good night, close eyes, and fall into the abyss.

UNLESS SHE HEARD JACK'S VOICE, Raelyn ignored landline phone calls. They were never for her. They were either robo calls about never-ending, upcoming elections, or they were for her parents. But that time, it was Angelica's voice on the machine. Rae had been declining her texts. It wasn't intentional, necessarily, just her typical avoidance when situations were messy. There had been the uncomfortable opera weeks before. There had been the Pet Lover's Club and stealing Megan and Cierra from her. There had been Miss Popular, Ginnie Harper, and the ultimate betrayal—the orange armband meetings.

But when she heard the squeaky voice in the kitchen, she knew her ex-*bff* finally must be desperate. She'd come back begging, tail between her legs. Rae picked up the phone, slightly triumphant. "Hello?"

"Hi, it's me. Angie." As if she didn't recognize the voice she's known since she was five; as if caller ID didn't read *Quinn*.

"Okay." Rae would keep the burden squarely on the caller.

"Um," Angie said quietly, "I need to talk to you."

"Oh."

"But not on the phone."

"Then why are we on the phone."

There was a pause. "Um, I wasn't in school today. I was sick." Another delay interrupted by a sniffle. "Gigi, we need to talk."

"You just said that."

"In private, I mean." A choking sound. "Look, I'm sorry, okay?"

Already, Rae was feeling like a horrible person.

Angie whispered, "There's something you'll want to know."

This piqued Raelyn's curiosity; nothing was more enticing than a good secret, if that was what Angie was getting at. "What?"

"It's what I can't tell you over the phone."

So the burden shifts to me, Raelyn noted, defeated but still dying to know. Life was so unfair. "Okaaay, so. . . ?"

"Can you come over? Please?"

"Right *now*?" Rae was already slipping on her boots—what a sucker.

"Uh-huh."

She made herself sound terribly bored. "I guess." She zipped up her coat.

"Oh, thank you!"

Rae mentally kicked herself as she pedaled around thin patches of snow on the sidewalks. She always stuck herself with the dirty work, jumping through the hoops, doing the favor—

even when the gain was for someone else. Even when she was on top, she ended up on the bottom. She wondered what was so important that it had to be told in person. A long overdue apology, perhaps, a kiss at her feet, a gesture of humility.

Angelica was waiting for her at the window with a finger to her lips. She let her inside in her baggy pajamas, lavender cupcakes bouncing all over the fabric.

"Dad, it's Gigi. She brought my homework," she called out. A little white lie, it barely counted. But Angie would confess it at church the very next Sunday, just in case, and dutifully follow through with extra Hail Marys. She would never lie to her parents.

"Make it quick, girls. We don't want Raelyn to get whatever you have."

The girls ran upstairs, and Angie shut the door. She stood with her back flush against it and again thrust her finger to her face. "Shh! You have to promise you will *never* tell!" Her face was puffy and pink.

"What is it?" This wasn't the *mea culpa* Rae was expecting.

The girls sat on the unmade bed. Angelica began to whisper, "You know how I'm not allowed to stay home alone yet, right?" Rae didn't respond. "Well, I didn't feel good this morning, and my Mom is away, so I went to work with Daddy like I sometimes do, right?" Rae didn't respond. "The police station always had a room with a cot, and—"

"I have no idea what you're talking about," Rae said.

"I'm trying to say," Angie began. She opened a top drawer

and turned to Raelyn with an orange armband. She dropped it in the waste basket, then turned to her again.

Rae shifted slightly. "That's what you had me come all the way over here for?" In truth, she was pleased that Angie seemed to have come around from the "dark side," but there was no need for gloating or drama. She wasn't about to applaud, if that's what Angie was after. Plus, this hardly amounted to an apology.

"There's more." Angie sat back down on the bed. "You knew my dad was transferred to the Compound, right?"

"No way."

"Way."

"When?"

"A while ago. I didn't want to tell you, 'cuz I know how you feel about Penelope and canines and everything." She looked frightened when she said this, as if Rae might bring an axe down on her head. But she didn't (not yet). "He got a huge pay raise. I've never been there."

Rae was ready to walk out. "Why are you even telling me this?"

"Until today." Angie's palms jumped up to cover her face, and then just as quickly fell, as if she'd never done it. She gulped. "You have no idea. No one does except the workers there. It's top secret."

Rae leaned forward. *Secret* carried an irresistible allure, even in such a distasteful context as this. "...*What* is?"

Angie glanced at the door. "First, there's a tall wire fence with metal knots along the top. My dad has a code to get in. A guy in a hard hat tells my dad that construction's finally done. He's nervous he'll get in trouble because of some delay. Daddy says, You'll have to take it up with Ollie. That's Chief Jerkins."

"I know that."

"Anyway, in the security building my dad gives me this lecture." She lowered her voice to a faint whisper. "I have to stay in a small room. If I need to use the bathroom, he'll *arrange* for it."

"That's messed up," Rae said, borrowing her brother's phrase. Then Angie whispered something directly in her ear.

"No *way!*"

"*Shush.*" Angelica eyed the door again.

"Like a *prisoner?* Has your dad gone crazy?"

"There's more," Angie continued. "So there I am locked in this room. And I hear my dad on the phone, but I can only make out a few words." She shut her eyes to better access her memory. "Something about the 'pit'. And 'ready to roll.'"

"What does it mean? What's the 'pit'?"

"No clue. But there's a window in the room, and it's painted black. I scratched a little section so I could see outside." Her face went pale. "It's not what people think."

Rae's eyelids closed. Then they opened. Then they closed and opened again, but nothing had changed. ". . .What do you mean?"

Angie grabbed her hands and held them tightly in her own, her gaze on the interlocked fingers between their laps. "Gigi, there will never be visiting hours. When I asked my dad, he laughed." Her hands began to tremble. "And on and off, I heard this strange wailing sound. Like a siren somewhere, or a high wind. Then I realized."

The girls fell into complete silence. The normal rhythms of thought were way off, like an at-risk, irregular heartbeat. Unlike Rae, who had sprouted upward like a bean, Angie hadn't grown much over the past year. Curled up, she was a pale pink mouse to her towering friend. A thin trickle curved down her cheek and her eyes were watery slits, barely open.

"Stop." Rae clamped her ears like a vise, her fingernails digging into her own scalp. "Stop it!"

"Shush!" Angelica's fist came down on Rae's head. "Shut *up!*" She fled to the door and pressed against it as if her petite form, cupcakes and all, could hold back a raging torrent.

Rae stared at the dizzying stars in front of her, feet dangling off the bed. Rubbing her head, she muttered, "Why did you do that?"

"You'd better go."

Rae proceeded to the door, massaging her scalp. But the door remained closed. "What are we going to do."

"Not me. I'd be grounded for life." Angie had gathered herself somewhat. "But you," she said flatly, staring down at her cupcake slippers, "I mean, I guess I can help a tiny bit, but that's all." Raelyn was nodding without realizing it. "And if you ever say *anything*, I swear, I'll never talk to you again. I will deny, deny, deny."

"I know."

"I will never let anything happen to my dad. Or my mom. Or me."

"I know."

"Sorry about your head."

"I know." In a surprise move, Rae brought her fist down directly onto Angie's crown.

"Oww-*wuh!*"

"Now we're even."

They met Mr. Quinn at the bottom of the stairs. "I was just about to check on you." His gentle voice had never before sent shivers. He lifted his daughter's chin. "You're getting worse, Pip, I can see it in your eyes. Maybe we should see the doctor." He glanced at Rae with equal concern. "You don't look so well, either. You're like a ghost—for *you*, I mean. Come on, I'll take you home."

Rae opened the front door. "I have my bike," she called as she rushed out. She pedaled home to the sound of Penelope crying out for her and a painful lump rising on her scalp.

At home, Jackson's letter with the sixth and final clue lay lifeless on the foyer floor. She stepped over it, unopened, and trudged upstairs. She lay on her bed like dead wood through dinner and waited for dusk to disappear into an early night.

Ever since Penelope was taken away, her once reliable Glitter had diminished to the slenderest of pickings. Each night, she waited patiently for the few lackluster flecks to dawdle onto the scene, only to quickly fizzle out and disappear. Still she canvassed the area, hanging on, never losing hope. But that night, after hearing Angelica's dreadful secret, her precious Glitter had been snuffed out completely. This was the moment when it all changed. For the first time in her life, there was nothing but dark-ness. She stared into the void.

And then she fell.

Strangely, from somewhere among the murky depths, small whispers arose:

Penny, can you hear me down here?

Why, yes, I believe so! Is that you, Raelyn?

Yes, it's me. You sound so small.

Yes, we are very small, indeed. I can barely smell you.

You and I, we're flip sides of the same coin.

Sorry?

That we're connecting right now by our thoughts; it's proof we're part of each other.

I suppose you're right!

Maybe we even share some DNA. Deoxyribonucleic acid, we learned about it in science.

I'm afraid you're breaking up, my dear. Can you repeat?

Hello? . . . My Lady, are you there? . . . Hello?

PENELOPE'S BELLY GROWLED, and no one was there to fill it. From one morning to the next, the twisting and contracting of her ab-domen never ceased—even after the feeding frenzy, the moment each day that she and all the others bit and scratched their way over each other for the scrap of a meal. Imagine that, and she such a proper lady. As primitive and vulgar as it was, this was the moment each day that she lived for. And the moment each day that, in turn, kept her alive.

At night, they crammed together for whatever warmth they could share. Some whimpered, some wailed. Some, like herself, kept silent. But they were all waiting for that euphoric, fleeting moment to arrive the next day, when they would fight among themselves for the remaining morsels. Waiting for their coats to grow to warm their exposed flesh. Waiting for their families to come and take them home.

Penelope waited for Raelyn. Rae had made a promise. She would never leave her in a place like this. Any day now, she would appear with her sunshine face, her herb-scented hair and joyful greeting, "Helloooo, My Lady!" Penny's life was becoming a series of things forgotten. She forgot about her special necklace, their Friday night sleepovers, leaping for T-R-E-A-T-S. But she never completely forgot that, in fact, there were things she was forgetting, things receding into fuzziness, buried amidst pangs of unquenchable thirst. If she vowed to remember anything at all, it was to hold onto memories of her beloved sister and the promise she had made.

CHAPTER 12

A Bucket, A Plan, And The Boy With The Swagger

I DREADED THE BOTTOMLESS PIT *so much that I began forcing it upon myself just to get it over with. If I was stuck with this dream, I would at least have it on my own terms. I cut to the chase, fast forwarded to the climax (or the depth, really). Forget the trivial red ball, my brother's dramatic warnings— just me helicoptering my arms at the edge and toppling into darkness. It no longer scared me because I controlled it. I forgot all about the Glitter; it had long abandoned me.*

I recognized the absurdity. Still falling? How many weeks now, how many months? Wouldn't I be hungry? So the family tossed me an apple, an orange, a slice of pizza—and I survived. Never mind physics. I was six. I wouldn't study physics until high school, when I learned that Isaac Newton's apple would never catch up with the weight of my body, no matter how much time passed; that under the sole influence of gravity, all objects free fall at the same rate of acceleration toward the center of the Earth.

The dream became predictable and plotless. It occurred to me that a hole in the Earth such as the one I was falling through would be full of tree roots. I began noticing thick, wooded growth protruding from the walls. In the midst of my rather boring descent, I grabbed hold of a sturdy root. For the first time in months, I came to a dizzying stop. Wow! Was it really as simple as this? Why didn't I reach out sooner? I asked myself. I grabbed another root above me, then another. They formed a ladder of sorts. I began to climb up.

It was much slower traveling against gravity than with it. Again, I didn't know the scientific formula, but logic told me that, if I'd been falling straight down at a whirling speed for months on end, it would take a lifetime to climb back to the top.

As with any transition, the new rarely replaces the old at a precise moment. A period of flux occurs in which both converge awkwardly and illogically, until the old recedes and the new takes a more prominent role. So it was with my Bottomless Pit. Night after night, I visited myself on a split screen: On the left, I was still falling weightlessly through the abyss, whooosh! On the right, I was climbing up the tree roots, one hand, one foot, one hand, one foot, and so on. Exhausted, but a real trouper, still climbing. The left screen eventually faded and disappeared, leaving only my strong, calloused fingers and toes clawing upward.

I would be climbing to this day if those dreams had continued.

But fortunately, my subconscious lost interest. Reaching the top was a certainty. I had conquered the dream.

RAELYN HAD LONG AGO GIVEN UP on wondering why—why Daffy County would be doing such awful things—and Angie had never been particularly curious. But they both knew instinctively that there was no justifiable answer to that question. There was no why, there was only what to do about it.

Before they met to formulate a plan, bits and pieces visited Rae in her sleep. But the precise manner of execution would be a challenge. Enter *Happy Hollow*, the perfect place for secret planning. They sat on the bright yellow floor among oversized pillows.

"Gigi, where's your green?" Angelica spun a three-sixty in her Irish plaid. "Today is St. Patty's Day." She offered her green scarf, but it remained untouched on Raelyn's lap.

"Okay, so: I'll have to get into the Compound again," Angie decided while Rae took notes. "I'll try to memorize the daily schedule—it's posted in the office—and learn what all the buildings are." She stared at a spot below the polka-dot ceiling as she spoke, as if trying to imagine the layout of the place. "I'll draw a map for you."

Raelyn wrote, *Angie—Map*. "Get info from your dad, too."

"That'll be easy." Both knew how smoothly parents could be manipulated into sharing seemingly harmless information if one did it right.

"And I'll practice being you!" Raelyn pantomimed fancy

gloves running up her arms. They shared a laugh. She had often wondered what it would be like to be Angelica Quinn for a day—but not on a dangerous day like the one they were planning.

Angie grew serious. "That's as far as I go, though. After that, I'm done."

"I know, duh. You told me ten times."

"Three times."

"Six."

"Okay, five." For the first time since their falling out, Angie made their signature heart shape with her hands. Rae returned the sign with some reservation, a haphazard display of fingers and thumbs. It all seemed rather childish to her now.

They agreed that a *code name* was essential. Rae listed the suggestions, and they narrowed it down to two, one from each of them: D-Day, for Dogs Day, but with a *double entendre* on account of World War II (Rae's idea); and UN, for Under their Noses (Angie's idea). Angelica assumed that, as always, her choice would win out. This time, though, Rae insisted. It was her mission, after all.

At the D-Day Second Planning Meeting, under *New Things*, Angie had a lot to report. She learned from her father that he was no longer stationed at the Blundertown Compound on Friday mornings because he'd been promoted to Regional Director (another pay raise, she added). Now he oversaw compounds in neighboring counties.

"You mean there are *others?*" Rae had never considered this.

"I guess so." The guard now covering Friday mornings was

brand new, didn't know much, and had never met her. "So Friday morning is perfect." Then she unveiled her portfolio and announced, "Ta-da, The Map!"

The girls hovered over the drawing on the cheerful floor. It was awesome, because Angie was an artist. Rae's rendition would have been simple squares with triangle-hat roofs, the fence a row of Xs, the roads parallel lines. But on Angie's map, every detail was three-dimensional with shading and texture and lovely calligraphy: *"Groom Room", "Front Gate", "Back Fence", "Woods", "Food Area", "Storage Shed", "Barracks I", "Barracks II", and "Security Station (SS)".* Several buildings near the back were marked *"New Construction??"* because she didn't know what they were. One was very tall and narrow, and the other a small structure next to it.

Angie flipped to a second map called *"Your Room."* Again, the detail was exquisite, with labeling and colors. There were two cots, the front one crossed out with a big "X" *("Night Guard!"),* the second with a redhead in bed, labeled *"You".* As Rae was admiring the impressive drawings, Angie quickly rolled them up and forced them into her hands. "Take these, and never bring them back here."

They had accomplished so much in only a week. But the biggest part of The Plan remained a mystery: What was Raelyn supposed to do once she got there? It wasn't enough for her to see whatever she might see and then report it. First, no one would believe her. Second, and more importantly, she would be suspended from school if she told her teacher, grounded for life if she told her parents, and sent to juvie jail if she told the police. This was a suicide mission. Not to mention it would crush her folks with, not one, but both of their kids "away for a while."

There had to be a way to document the goings-on in the Compound, whatever they were. But as Angie explained, Rae would be thoroughly searched on both the way in and out. It was impossible to sneak a recording device onto the grounds. So while they had their Code Name, lovely drawings, and a lot of useful information, and while Rae was getting good at being Officer Quinn's daughter, they'd hit a wall.

That changed two days later, after school. The girls removed their boots in the Quinns' garage. A trash can and two litter boxes were cluttering the floor near a stack of metal containers.

Rae asked, "What are those?"

"Food pails." Angie hopped up the steps and opened the door. "Come on in."

"Wait." The stack contained a dozen or so identical tin buckets with handles, ready to topple over. Rae released the top one and turned it in her hands.

"What are you doing?" Angie gasped. "Those are my dad's. For the. . .you know. They keep needing *more*."

"Why?"

Angie didn't answer.

Rae rummaged through her backpack, pulled out a ruler, and began measuring. Angie peeked into the house several times. "Eight inches across the top, nine high, and—" the bucket clanked as she flipped it upside down— "about six and a half at the bottom. Remember that." She tucked the ruler back in her bag. "Any idea when your dad is taking these?"

"Could be any time. They've been here all week."

"Let's hope we have a few days. I don't have Technology until Tuesday." When she saw the clouded, freckled face she added, "I'll explain later." It was satisfying to outwit Angelica just a little.

On Tuesday, Raelyn was prepared. She entered her Technology class and sat among her classmates at her usual work bench.

"Alright, listen up," Mr. Hanson said once the murmurs settled. "This is the last day to finish your boxes. For those who are done, we'll have a sneak peek at the next project." He paused for "oohs" and "ahhs," but none came. "So let's get our safety goggles and get to work."

Rae located her initials on a metal box on the table along the back wall. Her box was finished, but it gave her a pretext to wander. The majority of the class had followed Mr. Hanson to the other side of the spacious room, where he was showing them a wooden birdhouse lit up by a tiny solar panel. She acted quickly—darted to the materials table and grabbed an uncut sheet of thin metal. She measured and snipped a piece of twine, knotted it onto a pencil and rotated from the center, forming a circle on the flat piece. The metal was pliable, but too thick to cut without special scissors. She had no choice. She combed through the Industrial Materials drawer and pulled out a sturdy pair. Glancing in the teacher's direction, she proceeded to cut along the pencil markings, roughly seven and a half inches in diameter.

"Miss Devine, what are you doing over there?" She turned, hiding the metal piece behind her back. She was in an undesignated area and in clear violation of class rules. Plus, she'd forgotten to put on safety goggles, an automatic one-day suspension from class.

"I was just. . .looking for. . . ." All eyes were on her. Gil Richmond was suddenly a few feet away, off to the side. Her hair was surely a mess. Mr. Hanson was approaching. There was no way to hide the circle or explain it.

The teacher's scruffy beard was now directly in front of her. Maybe he wouldn't see it, but of course he did. "What is this?" He examined it. "Did you do this?" Again, she had no response. No lie, no excuse, no crazy story: *Look, a spider!* So this was what being caught with your hand in the cookie jar meant. This would cost her a failing grade. And worse.

"I made it." She hadn't opened her mouth. It was someone else's voice. "I'm sorry, Mr. Hanson. I shouldn't have done it." It was Gil Richmond. She stared at him, thoroughly confused. But his focus was on the beard. Gil had the metal disk in his hand. She hadn't even seen it happen.

"Well, Gil, I'm surprised and disappointed." Note the first-name basis for the AP's son. "And Miss Devine," he nodded, "I apologize." He scribbled something and handed it to Gil. "You'll take this referral to the AP office."

Why? Why had Gil covered for her? He never even looked at her. At the end-of-class buzz, she left baffled—and thoroughly relieved, which made her feel even guiltier. But what about the disk? She'd worked in a reckless frenzy, breaking all the rules in broad daylight under the teacher's nose, that's how critical it was. She had to get it back that day!

She stalled near the AP office, hoping Gil would appear, but he didn't. What an irony: She had purposely avoided him for five months (who was counting), and now he was the one person she desperately needed to see—and he was nowhere to be found. For the rest of the day, she scoured the halls between classes. She saw literally everyone, but no Gil.

At the next D-Day meeting that afternoon, they got down to business. Under *New Things*, the list read: (a) Gil has, *must get!!!*; (b) study for D-Day Test; (c) *date??*

"It's got to be this Friday," Angie announced.

"No way."

"Way."

"Why?"

"Because Daddy's taking those food pails in on Thursday. I heard him. There's a new truckload arriving that afternoon."

"Truckload of what?"

Angie looked down. "Of—"

"Dogs?"

"Yep."

"*More?*"

"From other places, I don't know. But that's what he says."

"But we *can't* do it Friday. Gil has my thing, and I haven't even seen him. Plus we have an English test."

"But if we are, quote-unquote, 'sick' that day," Angie's fingers formed parentheses, "we can make it up."

Rae wrote, *Friday!!* in her notebook and spun frantic ink circles around it. "But what if Gil won't give it back?"

Angie shrugged. "He *has* to." So easy for her to say.

They focused on the D-Day test. They wrote test questions on index cards with the answers on the back, one question per card: multiple choice, true/false, fill in the blank, change it up.

"Pip?" Mr. Quinn was knocking on the door. Both girls stiffened.

"Yeah, Dad?"

He opened the door. They were sprawled across patterned throw pillows with dozens of index cards scattered about. "What on Earth are you girls working on?" His smile was cheery and bold.

"Umm—"

"We have a test," Rae told him.

"Yeah. We're studying for a test." True.

"When is it?"

"Friday. It's a big test." Also true, as Angie would never lie to her parents.

"Huge."

He invited Raelyn to stay for dinner. They had a long way to go. They studied all evening for the Big Test, Angie reading the questions aloud and Rae answering. By Friday, she needed to score a hundred percent. She had to memorize Angie's maps, the morning schedule, and a whole lot more. She also would be tested on Quinn family trivia that might come up. But as Angie kept reminding her, after that she was on her own.

Question 1: What's the new officer's name?
>   *a. Officer Mudd*
>   *b. Officer Budd*
>   *c. Officer Crudd*
>   *d. Officer Smith*
>   *e. None of the above*

Question 2: True or False: The Groom Room is on the left if you're walking in from the Front Gate.

Question 3: Daily feeding time is:
>   *a. 9:15*
>   *b. 9:45*
>   *c. 10:15*
>   *d. 10:30*
>   *e. None of the above*

Question 4: Which of these is not searched at the Front Gate?
>   *a. Pockets*
>   *b. Lunch bag*
>   *c. Socks*
>   *d. Shoes.*
>   *e. None of the above*

Question 5: How many trips will the Guard (probably) take to feed the dogs?

a. 2

b. 4

c. 5

d. 8

Question 6: *What must you convince the Guard to do?*

(*short answer:* _____)

Question 7: *What time do we each get there, and where do we hide?*

Question 8: *How will you sneak in your phone?*

Question 9: *How should you act sick:*

a. *vomit/trips to bathroom*

b. *cough*

c. *look miserable*

d. *moan*

e. *all of the above.*

Question 10: *Where do we go when we're done?*

(*short answer:* _____)

Question 11: *Where are the Quinns going for spring break?*

a. *Paris*

b. *Florida*

c. *Las Vegas*

d. *Nowhere*

And so on.

On Wednesday morning, Rae spotted Gil cruising the hall ahead of her with a couple other boys. She sped up.

Angelica picked up her pace. "Wait up—where are you going?"

"I've gotta run. See you later." Rae took off, weaving among students until she was directly behind Gil. "Hey," she called to him.

"Hey." He kept walking, didn't look at her.

"Do you have my. . .thing?" She was at his side.

"What thing?"

"You know what I mean."

"No clue."

"You're a jerk." The other two boys snickered. "I need it."

She kept following him and refused to fall behind. Eventually, he stalled at the door to his next class until they were sufficiently alone. "Meet me at the park," he mumbled, looking the other way.

"What time?"

"I dunno. . .three?"

"OK. And bring it, please."

Rae was there a few minutes early. Her boots scuffed the hard, sandy patch under the swing. It was soon 3:04, and not a sign of him. He was toying with her: payback time. See what you get when you dis someone? It comes back to bite you. The minutes passed slowly, and when she looked again, it was 3:07. Her hair formed a wall on either side, enclosing her in failure. She knew she couldn't let a single teardrop fall, because there would be no end to them. She would drown in a puddle of mud at her own feet. What a way to go.

For the first time, she realized she was all alone in this affair. Angie could only help so much. Mr. E was gone. Jack was useless where he was. Her mother was a Stone Wall of No, which meant her father was, too. They'd rejected Doc Goodman's assistance when they had the chance. Penelope appeared in her mind, her marble eyes pleading directly into the pit of her soul. She heard her whimper. A heavy drop landed smack between her boots. Then another.

"Here you are." It was Gil.

She wiped a sleeve across her face. "You're late."

"I was waiting over there, in that—round thing." He pointed to the gazebo across the field.

"Do you have it?"

"I do."

She hopped off the swing and presented him with an open palm. "Then give it to me, please." He didn't answer. She needed it right there and then. She had to finish it and get it back to the Quinns' garage by the next day, or it would be too late. "I said *give* it to me."

He reached inside his coat, but his hand remained there. "What is it, anyway?"

"It's—it's just what it looks like."

"A metal circle?"

"Uh-huh."

"What's it for?"

"None of your business."

"Why do you want it so bad?"

"It's mine, that's all. Now hand it over."

"Tell me what it's for, and I'll give it to you."

". . .I can't tell you."

"Then I can't give it to you." His hand reappeared empty, his face smug.

It was a draw. She had no leverage. If she didn't cave, it was check mate: game over, her king slain and Penelope, too. She tried to read him without looking directly into his eyes, the path to the secrets of the heart. Could she possibly trust him? He was the only one who had shown up twice for the Pet Lover's Club, after all. And she had no choice. "Okay, then. I'll. . .I'll let you in on something if you promise not to tell anyone."

"Okay."

"Okay is not good enough."

"Promise."

"Full sentence, please."

"I promise."

"That I will not tell a single soul. . . ."

"That I will not tell a single soul. . . ."

"For as long as I live. . . ."

Gil rolled his eyes. "For as long as I live."

"And if I do, then I, Rae, will tell the whole world. . . ."

He scratched his neck and glanced around lazily. "And if I do, then you, Rae, will tell the whole world. . . ."

"About a certain bus ride in Kindergarten. . . ."

He stared at her. "You're kidding, right?"

"I'm not." She was absolutely bluffing. She couldn't and

would never be *that* cruel. He probably knew that. But she was playing her only card.

"Huh." He looked down at his feet and shook his head. "You're really something."

"So are you." But her shoulders sank, and she picked at her cuticles. "Just give it to me."

"I suppose you forgot that I *saved* this stupid piece of crap for you. Huh?" He pulled the disk out from his chest. "That I *covered* for you and got *lunch detention* because of you."

"...You got *lunch detention*? I thought—"

"Well, you thought wrong." He flipped his hair off his brow. "Everybody does."

"Oh." She wasn't even sure what he meant by that. She changed the subject. "So is Prince at the, you know."

"No."

It had been a rhetorical question, a convenient space filler. Every registered dog was there. "Where is he?"

His eyes reminded her of almonds. "At my grandma's house. She lives out of state."

"You're lucky."

"It's not luck," he corrected, "it's money. Two thousand dollars. We bought his way out."

There he goes again, boasting about how rich they were. But her eyes grew large with shock. "How? When?"

"Just before they closed the borders. You know, when you could pay your way out of this *insanity*."

She didn't know. Her parents had never told her. She had

never seen it in the newspaper. She was back to pivoting on the swing. He had never told her either, by the way, and something didn't add up. "Wait a second. How did you know to leave? How did you know they were going to close the parks and everything else?"

He acted like it was obvious. "My mom's an AP. My dad's a banker." Brag, brag, brag. "You follow the money." Such a smart-alecky, grown-up thing to say. "You follow school policy. They saw it coming."

Her own father was a politician, and yet there'd been no trace of foreshadowing in the Devine home. She pictured her dad, a large man and yet so small, nearly invisible sometimes. Her dismay left her speechless. She instantly shifted her suspicions back to Gil, whose story still didn't add up. "Why did you come to those stupid club meetings, then, if Prince wasn't even here?" she demanded.

"*Some* people care about more than just themselves, you know."

A car drove past, the only sound other than the shifting of the sand beneath her feet. She imagined Prince, so handsome with his full beard and intelligent eyes. "You could've at least let us say good-bye."

"I tried. You could've at least responded."

"You mean. . ." *The green envelope, the uphill writing. It had never been about a date.*

"What did you *think* it meant?" The way he glared at her, she could have been a circus freak. "Prince was leaving the next day."

"I know that, duh. What did you *think* I thought?"

He was on the swing next to hers, both scuffing clumsy patterns in the dirt. How could she have been so stupid? They were eleven, after all, and no one writes letters like that. It had never been about her. It was always Penelope. And why not? Rae truly was the biggest loser on the planet.

"Well, Penelope is. At the Compound, I mean." She paused. "And that's what the metal circle is for."

"Here." He handed over the disk. "Was that so hard?" He scribbled something on a scrap of paper. "Whatever you're up to—" he handed it to her— "call me crazy, but I happen to care about her, too."

She watched him sail down the gravel path in his springy-tipped sneakers. She read the scrap of paper, a minty gum wrapper. It was his cell phone number.

"GOT IT," SHE REPORTED TRIUMPHANTLY to Angie that evening at their final D-Day meeting. Yet another Gil story that she kept under wraps: The list kept growing. The metal circle fit snugly three quarters down one of Officer Quinn's buckets, creating a perfect hiding place at the real bottom. "And here's the address for the Welfare Society that my brother told me about." She showed Angie her notebook. "It's an agency that's in charge of a bunch of things, including animal safety. He learned about it in Civics, but they don't teach that anymore." Lucky for her, he was a packrat. He'd stashed years of notebooks under his bed and had a nearly photographic memory of their contents. During the last visit, he'd told her exactly where to look.

She passed the D-Day test with flying colors. Angie popped a shiny star on her forehead and ripped up the index cards into teeny pieces. All evidence destroyed. They began a list called *Things That Could Go Wrong*, with the idea that anticipating such matters would be helpful. But they very quickly realized that the list would be endless. The fact was that more things could go wrong than right, and the consequences of a failed mission, at least for Rae, would be disastrous.

"Let's not do that." Angie tossed the paper aside. "Let's do the hair!" This would be the most fun of all. In the mirror, Angie cut swatches of her ginger hair from the underside. Rae grabbed the French beret from months before and the super glue. Together they attached the locks to the front inside rim of the hat, forming a row of bangs. "Try it on!"

Raelyn twirled her masses of coarse hair into a bun and forced the beret over it. Angie jiggled the bangs until they hung uniformly over the forehead. "Wait," she said as if she were asking a question, her hand reaching for the scissors. She snipped meticulously here and there. "Wait." She fitted the matching beret on her own head. "Come here, Gigi—I mean *Angie!*" The two girls stood side by side at the mirror. Two identical faces stared back at them.

Well, not quite. Rae did not make a good redhead. Her skin tone, her thick eyebrows and lashes—it was all wrong. But it had to be good enough. She saw her "twin's" image fade, leaving her own flawed reflection. Angie's role was coming to an end. Friday morning, it would all be on Raelyn.

CHAPTER 13

Plan "A"

I WAS OFTEN WITH MY FAMILY *on a dangerous mission. My mom or dad would be in the front passenger seat, Jack and Penelope in the back. But here is the thing: I was always the driver. I was eight, but I was the master driver, and no one thought anything of it. I knew how to downshift up steep hills, and make sharp turns to avoid unexpected origami birds and caped demons with fluorescent eyes. I swerved skillfully around pot holes, any of which could be a Bottomless Pit from which there was No Way Out. I never crashed once.*

In this particular dream, our mission was to take secret photographs while visiting an elderly couple who was out to get us and abscond with the Golden Box of Evidence. I got us all safely to the Old Folks' Home on the Hill. They were wrinkly and all smiles, but we weren't fooled by their false-toothed grins. Danger lurked, and everyone in my family lacked courage except me. Wearing my spy glasses downstairs, I spotted the Golden Box of

Evidence in the farthest room on the second floor. It was just a matter of getting it out of the house under the Old Timers' noses. Jack tiptoed up the winding staircase, bopping forward, then backward, on each step. A moment later, he slid down the walnut banister and delivered the Golden Box into my able arms. My spy glasses took photographs—flash! flash!—while the others exchanged goodbyes. The Devines hopped into my silver convertible, and, at top speed, I tore down the roller coaster road into safety, dodging pot holes and bottomless pits all along the way. Mission accomplished.

ON D-DAY MORNING, the girls doctored up their sick stories to the parents. Angie didn't really lie because, in fact, she *did* have an awful stomach ache. They timed their separate arrivals perfectly, Rae arriving by bike and hiding in the woods by the *Front Gate*, and Angie dropped off by her father shortly afterward. It was late March, the air crisp and heavy. They conferred briefly in their frost-covered hideout, where Rae adjusted the beret with the phony bangs.

"You'll never guess what happened," Angie exclaimed. "I almost didn't make it here. Of all days, *today* my dad decides I'm old enough to stay home alone. He said it didn't make sense for me to be here when he wasn't." She found herself having to argue against her own self-interest; how ironic. "Imagine arguing that you're *not* mature enough and you need a grown-up. But, Gigi, I was so convincing! I'm seriously thinking about acting school." Flickers of confidence gleamed as she spoke, and Rae saw that she wasn't joking. "I mean—" Angie winced— "you know, some day." She fiddled with the row of bangs on Rae's forehead. "Good luck—*Angie!*"

"Thanks, Angie."

Angelica made the foolish heart shape, but Rae's arms remained at her sides. For her, childhood had ended that day. Angie gave her a nervous hug. They both recognized it for what it was: the kiss of death. For beyond this point, Officer Quinn's daughter would throw her friend under the bus to protect herself if need be, and both of them knew it.

Rae walked alone to the *Front Gate*. She took a deep breath and pushed the buzzer.

"Who's there?"

"Me, Angie. Umm, Pip."

"Be right there." A short man in uniform approached and unlocked the massive gate. "*You're* Pip?" He stared at her. Then a gold tooth showed as he smiled. "I'm Officer Budd. Not feeling well, huh?" Rae coughed. "Your dad says you know the deal."

"Yeah."

"Pockets."

She flipped her pockets inside out.

"Lunch." She opened her bag, and he poked around with his fingers: the important sandwich, an apple, carrots.

"Shoes." He inspected the insides and she wiggled her stockinged feet.

"Hat."

She froze. Already! They had not thought of this, but of

course! Instinctively, she pulled the sides of the beret down in an effort to preserve the bangs and her life. "Um," she said, "my— my hair is. . .really dirty."

"Not to worry."

"No, really. Can I please not?"

To Officer Budd, she was one more self-conscious pre-teen with panic-stricken eyes. The last thing he wanted was to embarrass his brand-new boss's daughter. "Listen, never mind." His spot of gold showed. "I don't make these crazy rules. Come on in," he added, and winked. Another grown-up winker.

She followed him down a dirt path, identifying everything around her thanks to the impeccable map. There was the *Groom Room* to her left. They passed the *Storage Shed* next. The large *Barracks I* was up ahead, with *Barracks II* behind it. A pungent odor hung in the air. For as much planning as they'd done, nothing in her life experience led to any identification of the foul odor. She squeezed her nostrils closed.

"Sorry," he apologized. "You get used to it. Damn canines, stink something awful." His head was entirely flat on top from a buzz cut. "I only work here."

Usually the real thing is more spectacular than any artistic rendition. But in that place, Angie's pretty little drawing trumped reality. It was all dull shades of brown and gray: the fences, the buildings, the dirt road. Even the sky was dismal. The place appeared empty. It was inconceivable that hundreds of dogs lived there. Where were they, and how would she ever photograph them?

Lastly, there it was in the distance, shielding the forest beyond: the tall smoke stack slicing through the fog like a dagger.

"This way," he said. "You know."

Had she been looking around too much, she wondered; how did Angie's hair look? she worried. She followed him through the front door of the SS and up a flight of stairs. To the left sat a cluttered desk with a computer screen; a large window over-looked the grounds, and there was a clock on the wall. A ciga-rette was slowly burning in an ashtray. Posted to the side was the daily schedule, marked in ten-minute increments. She knew that the scribbled note next to 10:00 a.m. would say "Groom" and at 10:30 would say "Feed." She made a mental note of where the bathroom was.

Officer Budd grabbed a key from a wall hook and escorted her to the right of the stairs. This was *Her Room,* exactly as Angie described it: two cots with sheets and blankets, a lamp, a footstool, and a small window behind a sheer curtain.

"Give a holler if you need anything. Like I said, sorry, but I don't make the rules." He locked her in.

She stood completely still. She couldn't believe she was actu-ally in the inner sanctuary of the SS, breaking laws, being some-one else. There was no clock. She tiptoed to the window and gently pushed the curtain to the side. Sure enough, in the upper corner was a tiny patch. Angie had chipped away at the black paint with her fingernail, clearing a portion of the glass. Rae moved the footstool to the window, stepped up, and peered through. She watched and waited. She found herself strangely calm one minute and trembling out of control the next —no rhythm, no reason, just a senseless ping-pong of random reflexes. It was only about nine in the morning, she guessed, yet it already had felt like an entire day. She began scraping the paint with her nail to expand her view, careful not to overdo it.

She remembered she had a job to do: Somehow, she had to convince Officer Budd to leave her door unlocked. She tapped on the door. "Hello?"

"Yeah, Pip?"

"I'm gonna throw up!" she moaned. Her door was opened instantly, and she ran past him to the bathroom. She groaned and gagged. She flushed, ran water in the sink, and gargled. She adjusted Angie's bangs in the mirror, practiced a pallid, sickly expression and exited.

"Stomach bug?"

"I guess," her voice was weak. He locked her back in. Who needed acting classes?

For a time, the only sounds were a squeak of the chair and a manly clearing of the throat. She guessed he would be finishing another cigarette. When the phone rang, she pressed her ear to the door and listened: something about "efficiency" and working "like magic." She repeated the vomit scenario. The plan was that, after the third trip to the bathroom, she would ask him to keep the door unlocked. Third time's a charm, they say.

"Groomer here." It was a woman's voice on speaker.

"Roger," Officer Budd replied.

"Infestation duty."

"Tell me about it. My application's already in for the night shift. They get to sleep instead of deal with this crap."

"Roger, my man."

A buzzer followed. At the window, Rae saw a uniformed woman heading toward Barracks I. She opened the door, and a group of dogs exited. How thin and mangy they were! There were ten or fifteen of them, all sluggish and slow. Some were limping, and there were no wagging tails. The groomer closed the barracks door halfway on one of them, and a piercing yelp shot across the yard. "Stay, you mutt," she shouted. To the others, she ordered, "Come, flea bags!" chasing them toward the *Groom Room*. It would be impossible to know whether Penelope was among them. They followed the woman inside. After quite a while, the door opened and they marched out. To her horror, she saw that they were even more emaciated than before. She realized instantly that they'd been shaved of all their fur. Their coats had given them more bulk, the illusion of mass and weight, but they were scarcely more than bone.

Her third trip to the bathroom was not an act. The vomit was real, the stabbing ache in her gut real—the cold sweat, dizziness, watery eyes, all real.

"Wow. You alright?"

"No!" She glared at him. "I mean, I'm just. . .sick, okay?"

"I'll tell you what," he offered. "I'll leave this door unlocked for you. The bathroom's there if you need it." He added helplessly, "No need to mention this to your dad. He'll be here in about forty-five minutes to take you home."

THE THING AT THE EDGE OF BLUNDERTOWN

He saw the groomer out and returned to his desk. Raelyn pulled off another minor bathroom trip in order to see the clock: 10:28. Bucket Time had come.

As soon as she heard his footsteps down the stairs, she perched herself at her watch post. He was planting the pails in a row in the *Food Area* and pouring a small amount of dog food in each. Next, he would take them to the barracks several at a time. As soon as his back was to her, she fled out of her room and down the stairs. She sprinted across the dirt road to the buckets and scanned them for the small heart she had marked at the bottom of the special one, all the while glancing obsessively in the direction from which he'd be returning. She searched one pail after another. Halfway down the line, an awful thought occurred to her: What if hers was among the ones he'd already delivered? Another thing the girls hadn't contemplated. Then she saw it: the tiny scribble in permanent marker. She grabbed the prized container, ran back to the SS building, and crouched behind the door in the foyer. Officer Budd appeared in the distance.

She scooped through the dry morsels until she reached the false metal bottom. Her fingers fumbled along the edges of the disk that she'd skillfully fit so snugly into the pail. Another mistake. If she could do it again, she'd make it a looser fit so it would release easily. But sometimes life doesn't give you second chances, and this was one of them. She shimmied her thumb nail under the edge of the false bottom and slid it along the circumference, prying as she moved along. There was no give at all. She imagined Officer Budd discovering her here, squatting behind the door with a bucket of dog food. The life she knew would be over.

She peeked out. He had reached the *Food Area* and then was gone again with more pails in hand. She dumped the kibble onto the floor and again shoved her thumb nail into the razor thin space, pulling and maneuvering. While she did so, she stared absentmindedly at the tiny pile on the floor, doing the math. If there were as many dogs here as they predicted and only twenty-eight buckets, this small amount of food was meant to feed ten or more. No wonder they were so skinny. She was getting a feel for it with her thumb, on the cusp. Suddenly, it shifted. Finally! She gave a forceful tug upward and the false bottom escaped from its perfect fit. And there it was, like a pearl in her hand: her cell phone, good as new. She slipped it in her pocket and scooped the morsels back into the container.

When the coast was clear, she ran out to the dwindling line, left her pail among the others and sped back to relative safety. Her head was spinning from the adrenaline and near- misses, and from knowing that the hardest part of the plan still lay ahead.

Her thumb was throbbing and dripping blood. She wiped red droplets from the floor with a hasty sleeve. She would need to hide the metal piece where it wouldn't be found any time soon. She lifted the mattress at the foot of the bed and wove the disk between several springs until it lodged into place. Next, she powered up her phone. Wow, twenty-seven messages since yesterday morning? No kidding! There were texts, tweets, Instagrams and Snapchats. It felt like weeks since she and her phone had parted, but it had only been a day. A text from Gil that morning asked if today was "the day." (FYI, she was secretly relieved about the Gil thing, despite it having been the most embarrassing moment of her life. Besides, the last thing she needed just then was a boyfriend.) She was in the middle of a response when she mentally slapped herself: *Earth to Moron, Job to Do.*

Had she closed the door at the bottom of the stairs? Wiped up all the blood? She crept down the steps, saw no sign of him, shut the door, and checked for bright red dots. There were none, but there was a lone piece of dog food lying there, dead center for all the world to see. Many a critical mission was foiled by as small an oversight as this. She picked it up and (she would never, *ever* tell anyone this, except, foolishly, Gil) she popped it in her mouth and swallowed just as footsteps sounded. She tripped on the way upstairs and hopped in bed, stiff as a corpse. The door opened below.

The countdown began. Neon numbers flipped in her mind as nausea clutched onto her from the inside. The rest was dangerous lunacy. What had they been thinking? It sounded so simple: one, find a clever way to sneak a camera into the Compound; two, take photographs of the unspeakable goings on; and three, distribute the photos as proof to the outside world. But they'd never detailed exactly how to "take photographs"— nor could they have. No one had ever been in the position to do it. She closed her eyes and let the minutes crash over her like turbulent ocean waves as she struggled to stay afloat.

Finally, Officer Budd left the building again. She followed him through the spot on the window pane. It must have been eleven o'clock: roll call. The time had come which she, alone, could expose to the world. It was a calling and a duty she had taken on herself. And suddenly, she didn't want it. She didn't want to see, didn't want to know. For the first time, she longed to be in English class, taking a test right now, where the only problem she faced would be flunking it. Before this morning, a failed grade would have been a big deal. Now, it was mere child's play—a frivolity compared to what she was staring at.

Out came the dogs from Barracks I: a running stampede. Officer Budd was shouting at them and swatting, stick figures all. There were elderly dogs and puppies, some with large floppy ears that weighed down their burdened bodies, others with triangle ears that made them look perpetually happy—even in a place like that. But not a single tail wagged. Somewhere among them was her beloved Penelope. She peeled her eyes across the masses, searching for the shiny tan-and-black coat and the birthday collar. But the dogs had been stripped of their identities, reduced to a horde of starvation.

She pressed her phone flush against the cleared spot on the window. Her grip was firm and steady. I'm not really seeing what I'm seeing, she told herself. In truth, she was only seeing her electronics. It was the inanimate screen in her hand that was "seeing" the patch of glass, and in turn, it was the smudged pane that was witnessing the scene below. And all of this went first through the lenses of her glasses. So, she reasoned, she was four times removed, four distant steps from reality. She was seeing an illusion, nothing more.

But as she took the shots, the phone wobbled and her fingers shook. She was about to faint. She pressed the button several times. She could take no more.

She suddenly didn't recognize the small, bare room she found herself in. Where was she? What *was* this hideous place? His commanding boots stomped up the stairs, each step like a gun-shot. She opened her lunch bag and stuffed the contents of the sandwich into her mouth. She hid the slender phone between the bread, re-wrapped it and chomped fast. She stared straight ahead and breathed: *in, two three; out, two three. Chew, chew, swallow!*

A knock came at her door. "Everything alright, Pip?" It was the pleasant voice of a demon. How dare he address her by Angie's endearing nickname?

Vibrations traveled up her throat, and she heard a "yes."

"Your dad called. He'll be here in a couple minutes to run you home."

She jumped off the bed, grabbed her lunch and jacket, and started to leave.

He blocked her at the door. "You know the routine," he apologized as he opened her lunch bag. "Silly procedures, I know, but they must be followed." He fingered quickly through the items. He pulled out the sandwich to the sound of someone's heart pounding. "Like you could eat your lunch, right." He tucked the sandwich back in the bag and handed it to her. She showed her empty pockets, shoes and socks, and accompanied him to the *Front Gate*. "Hope you feel better." He unlocked it.

Once he was out of sight, she made a turn for the woods, where Angie was doing jumping jacks behind a tree. "It's about time!" she exclaimed, warming her hands. "It gets cold out here all alone. And so boring."

"Done," was all Raelyn could say. She tossed the hat with the glued hair into the trees, hopped on her bike, and was gone. Five minutes later, Mr. Quinn's police vehicle pulled up to his daughter waiting for him.

By noon, both girls were in school, reportedly feeling much better. Rae got her first zero on an assignment. *Failed,* it read.

But she didn't feel like a failure at all.

CHAPTER 14

How To Pass Inspection (With Tricks And Illusions)

MY MOTHER WAS OBSESSED *whenever company came with presenting a fantasy of what the day-to-day Devines really were. We would stuff bags of miscellany into closets and drawers, haul laundry baskets well out of sight, display the brass candlesticks. In my dream, I was in a large, echoey room with alabaster pillars and famous paintings on the walls in ornate frames.*

"Where are we?" I asked.

"Home."

AN ENVELOPE MARKED *Welfare Society* landed on a large, cluttered desk along with a stack of other mail. It had no return address. The director guessed it was from a child. She remained standing as she sliced open the envelope at the seam. The photos that spilled onto her desk were amateurish—out of focus and un-centered. Her first inclination was to toss them directly into the trash.

But one image caught her attention—an erect structure in the distance with a cluster of objects in front of it. One was a man who towered over the others. She drew the photo closer. They were four-legged animals of varying sizes, none reaching much above the man's knees, but unidentifiable. They were hairless like wet seals, the legs skinny like those of ostriches.

She flipped to the next photograph of these same creatures standing in perfect rows on rickety appendages. The third photo showed a skeletal figure with bowed head and tucked tail, a man standing over it with a club. She made out the grainy features, the eyes wide and vacant, the jaw clamped. It dawned on her that the peculiar animals were dogs.

She sank into the chair, picked up the phone, and ordered an investigation.

Word got out immediately.

Never underestimate the ingenuity and precision of a well-oiled murder machine. The Blundertown Compound's classified, internal memo reports that it is taking a seventy-two-hour hiatus to undergo a Quick Change—a total alteration of set and scenery. The chimney stops abruptly. Bleach pours out by the truckload, the dirt roads hosed down and neatly raked. The betraying odors dissipate with air fresheners, and a van of new prisoners arrives from out of county. There are a dozen poodles, all quite healthy, with curly coats and bountiful muscle and fat. Hold off on the routine grooming for now. Triple up their kibble portions and fill their water bowls. For now.

When the Welfare Society Investigative Team arrives at the Blundertown Compound, they are met with a smiling crew led by Angelica's father, Officer Ted Quinn. They also are met at the entrance by a small garden filled with roses, petunias, and geraniums, and a gardener clipping the shrubs. Even a yellow butterfly has found its way there. Never mind that it's barely spring; it's April Fool's Day.

Officer Quinn leads the Investigative Team on a limited tour of the premises. Of *course* we have nothing to hide, he seems to be saying; come right this way.

The Team follows him with their clipboards and pens to a fenced in playground called *Pooch Park*. Inside are a dozen frolicking poodles, each in a bright red bow, not a single rib showing. There are balls and toys and a small drinking pond.

"Snack time!" calls Officer Quinn. The poodles trot over to him with bright, excited eyes. He feeds one after another a bone-shaped treat and pats each on the head. He instinctively wipes his hand on the back of his trousers.

Come, let me show you their dorm, he suggests. The small building is immaculate, with two tidy rows of fluffy, individual beds with built-in pillows. Alongside each bed a water bowl is filled to the brim. You would imagine these residents enjoy a bedtime story each night.

And what about those two large buildings over there? someone on the Team asks.

More of the same, Officer Quinn explains. More state-of-the-art bedrooms, more bedtime stories. Would you care to see them?

If you don't mind. . . .

Mind? Not at all! He gives a heartwarming chuckle. But our guests might be sleeping; it's their nap time. We'll try not to disturb them, that's all.

Oh! No, please. There's no need. Not if it's their nap time.

You sure? You are more than welcome to see—

No, it's quite alright. The Team shifts gears. What about those two buildings in the distance over there? The small white one and the large tower?

Come, we'll show you. See, the small building here is the Spa. Our guests enjoy baths with warm water and bubbles in here, and they are hand dried with fluffy white towels. Egyptian cotton. The tower over here—it's a chimney, really—is where debris and garbage are disposed of. It keeps the Compound clean and pleasant, dirt and disease free. We're a one hundred percent germ-free facility.

The Team is impressed. Their notebooks are closed. Frankly, they are a bit embarrassed. What had they been expecting to see here, anyway?

Thank you for the most informative tour. We're sorry to have inconvenienced you.

Not at all! The honor is entirely ours. Feel free any time. We have an Open Door Policy here.

The Team is escorted to the Gate. They shake hands and part ways.

Investigation closed.

Jackson had always been a good magician. He could make things disappear before your very eyes: coins, playing cards, plastic jewels, you name it. The "trick," he confided in Raelyn, lay not so much in making an object disappear (for that was impossible) as in getting your audience to look the other way. "So when I wave my right hand overhead with a shiny quarter between my thumb and finger," he demonstrates, "your eyes follow. While the *real* action," he says, pausing for dramatic effect, "is happening—" his left hand flips open quietly at his side— "*here*." But though Rae honed in with razor sharp focus, she could never catch him in the act. And like any good magician, he never revealed exactly how he did it. She still saw things disappear before her very eyes.

So it had been on that day at the Blundertown Compound. The trick was to avert the inspectors' attention from the real action by directing it to an extraneous event—the fairytale dorm room that had been created precisely for this purpose. The trick was to create an appealing, plausible Alternate Reality that the inspectors would much prefer to the truth. The lovely garden, the woman with a twinkle in her eye and shears in her hands, the red bows, the bone-shaped treats, fluffy new beds and the "Spa" sign—all of these things were Jack's right hand waving a shiny, perfect coin overhead of a man in a wig.

CHAPTER 15

Jackson's Jolly Followers

EVEN WITH HER KEEN NOSE, *Penelope and I were trapped in a cave, lost. We wandered together aimlessly in my dream until we heard Jack's voice echoing from somewhere high above: "T-R-E-A-T! T, t, t. . . !" Penelope spun around and broke into a gallop, following the sonar trail of letters. I chased her tail, as it made a left turn out of sight.*

EIGHT YOUNG MEN IN GRAY TROUSERS and button-down shirts sat around a table. A man considerably older wore a blue uniform and stood at attention, a firearm in his holster. The leader of the gray group was Jackson Devine, Number 502734993. This was their fourth session, and they were psyched to get started.

On the table lay the following items: six pairs of scissors, fabric remnants of vibrant colors and patterns, straight pins, assorted threads, sewing needles, measuring tape, thimbles, and a stack of finished products.

"Alright, boys," Jackson announced, rolling up his sleeves, "let's get to it."

They dove in for their favorite fabrics and materials and began to sew.

The young men were hand-stitching neck scarves by the dozen: large, medium, and small. The scarves would be gifts for all the dogs who were currently imprisoned. Unlike themselves, however, the dogs had never violated any laws at all. This kind of blatant injustice rubbed these fellows the wrong way. They couldn't do much—at least while they were housed there—but they could do *something*.

Jackson was an optimist, convinced that, one day soon, the dogs would be freed. When that day came, the first thing they'd do, he guessed, would be to toss away the government collars with the despicable numbers. His idea was to give each of them something special to replace them with. They stored the growing number of bandanas for the pooches' return home. But when no one was watching, Jackson slipped his newly finished scarf into the back pocket of his trousers. It was long and made of silk, with dazzling streaks of color. The delicate, fluid patterns seeped through each other like water, a burst of rainbow tucked safely in his keeping.

There had been considerable red tape and resistance before his sewing club was formed. When he first presented the idea to his mates, they'd looked at him strangely for sure. They teased him relentlessly. But soon they came to see that he was dead serious and wasn't going anywhere (at least for a while), and neither were they.

Selling the idea to the Powers That Be was a greater challenge. They considered having him evaluated by the staff psychiatrist, who came on Tuesdays. But Number 502734993 charmed them and made his case, and eventually they endorsed the Jackson Sewing Club. What was the harm? The club was the first of its kind in the institution's seventy-five-year history.

Imagine these budding young tailors tangling their thread, pricking their fingers and thumbs, howling, "Son of a—*ouch*!" shaking their hands in the air, and sucking their fingers in pain, all while telling jokes, laughing, and concentrating. Over time, they became quite skilled, too. These would be the best memories they would have of the place. And they would remain so long after they left.

MEANWHILE, PENELOPE WAS DIGGING. Her calloused paws scrabbled at a furious pace, scooping the rocky dirt and flinging it frantically behind her. On either side of her was an endless line of other dogs digging, too. Together, they were digging the largest, deepest, longest hole any of them had ever dreamed of, the dirt flying behind them in a blinding spray. Big dogs, tiny dogs, young and old, all in a row, all furless and afraid, digging to the shouted commands of the guards.

To slow down meant a beating, or perhaps something worse—being taken away someplace. She had never seen those dogs again, impossible to imagine. She didn't know how she could dig one more inch, mow her paws one more time into the heartless soil, but somehow she did. She dared not contemplate beyond the moment. She dared never project into the imminent future—when her paws would comb through the rocky terrain for the last time, her last drop of energy depleted.

"Hello," a low voice murmured next to her. It was a Doberman Pinscher digging to her left. He was quite thin, of course, and a good deal younger than she, his sinewy musculature still intact. By the whiff of him, she guessed him to be in his prime.

"Hello!" she whispered.

"You know what we're digging, don't you?" he asked. She hadn't the faintest idea and really hadn't thought about it. *"We are digging our own graves,"* he said.

"No!" she stopped abruptly. *"That's not possible!"*

"Shh! Keep digging," he ordered, and she did. A guard approached, his eyes set on Penelope for several moments, and then moved on. The Doberman coughed. *"There's a group of us here planning an escape. We need your help."*

"Me?" Penelope was shocked. *"I'm nearly an old lady! Look at me. I'm skin and bones. What possible use could I be?"*

"We've watched you. You talk to no one. You're very discreet. We need those who can keep a secret," he explained. *"And for an old lady, you're a fine digger. We need efficient diggers."*

She blushed. *"Thank you. But my family will be coming for me soon,"* she explained. *"Raelyn promised. It was the last thing she said to me."* An obscure image crossed her mind of her tall, sweet sister with the herbal hair, bending down and enveloping her in a burst of love.

The Doberman shook his head. *"Your family doesn't know what's happening here. No one does."* He added, *"or wants to."*

"That's impossible! How can no one know?" No sooner did she say this, she recognized it for what it was: an admission of what she, herself, knew to be true. The tall chimney loomed before them, the stench of death as proof. She spoke on in disbelief: *"What about the community just over those trees? Surely, they must know what's going on right under their noses."* But Penelope was dizzy, the scoops of earth a blur amidst her forepaws.

"You can't wait for your family." The Doberman coughed again. *"Join us."* He waited for her response, but none came. He continued, his voice nearly inaudible even inches away. *"We've been digging a tunnel out. We don't call ourselves 'The Underground Squad' for nothing,"* he smiled. *"There's a long way to go. We can only work at night when the night guard is asleep."*

"He sleeps?"

"Fortunately, he does." The Doberman coughed a third time. My goodness, she realized, he was not at all well. She noticed how tired he looked around the jowls and the eyes. Imagine that— digging all night after digging all day on only a few kibbles of food. Pangs of admiration, guilt, and terror jumbled her brain as she clawed into the soil.

"Alright," she heard herself say. *"I'll do what little I can."* And from that moment on, she no longer recognized herself.

ALL ALONG THE EDGE OF BLUNDERTOWN, the bedroom curtains inch open silently in the early hours. Restless insomniacs tiptoe across the carpets in the dark, peering through the windows at the gray-violet skyscape. All is still. Momentarily, you make out a faint, curved line, thin as a pencil mark, outlining the edge of the woods. It is from that direction that the sounds come. Eerie, howling sounds, as if from a far-off, haunted house, they travel like radio waves over the forest canopy, past the newly erected fence, across the field and the children's swing sets, the sheds stocked with rakes and snow blowers. The sounds swirl and curve, muffling their way through the windows, seeping into feather pillows, lodging themselves into your dreams. You imagine the howling is a chorus. Harmonies of soprano, alto, tenor, and bass, soothing you to sleep like crashing waves on a summer night. But suddenly the uniform howling picks up tempo, a staccato of short notes screeching over layers of anxious, deeper tones. The music becomes a desperate pleading in the night, a frantic melody.

Then, just as suddenly, it stops.

"Harold?" An elderly woman turns on her bedside lamp, "Harold, there it is again!" she whispers. She taps his white-haired chest. An eye opens reluctantly, his snore becoming a groan. "Did you hear it?" she asks, relieved that he is finally awake, but worried. "Do *you* smell it, too? Or am I imagining things again?" She glances out the window from her bed. She swears she sees a faint trail of smoke in the distance.

"Mm." His lids settle back over closed eyes.

"*Harold!*" He sits up, mops his face with a veiny hand. His elbow supports him precariously. "What do you think it is?" Her voice is hoarse from the night.

"I don't know," he says. "Probably burning garbage. Go back to sleep."

"That's not garbage. It's different, a horrid smell, Harold." His soft snore is his only response.

When she turns back toward the window, the sky is clear, the trail gone.

At the edge of Blundertown, the thin curl of smoke mingles and colludes with the nighttime sky, diffusing into the clouds: *I'll take some, you take some, let's scatter our evidence away.* Invisible wisps make their way over to the rows of houses and through the windows, settling between the sheets, the miniscule hairs in your nostrils as you tuck yourself back into bed. You simply don't know, you tell yourself. It's not your business, but you wish it weren't so close to home. Little do you know that the neighbors are peeking out their windows too, telling themselves the same things before settling back into restless sleep.

In the morning, all is forgotten. Except by little Cindy, who molds play dough into four stubs and a chubby body, yellow into ears and blue into a wagging tail.

"Why do you say that, Cindy Lou?"

"Because, Mommy, that's what it is. Dogs crying."

CHAPTER 16

Will The Real Joan Robin Please Stand Up?

I DREAMED I HAD REACHED *the ninth wicket, my final destination on the croquet course. I aimed, took a deep, optimistic gulp, and clonk!—propelled my bright yellow ball directly through the stake with my mallet.*

"I won! I think I won!" I exclaimed while executing impressive victory leaps around my triumphant wooden ball. "Oh, yeah. Oh, yeah," I gloated.

"Not so fast." Dad was tallying up the points—25 for me, 24 for mom. "Mommy still gets her last turn." Behind me, my mother puffed a breath of magic into her hands and rubbed them together for the kill. She re-adjusted her feet and hips three times, eyeballing the trajectory from her ball to the final wicket with steely eyes, a competitive grin. She clutched her mallet and gave a masterful, steady swing. I watched her blood-red ball plunk

forward, a perfect advance. I held my breath. The ball was still traveling toward the finish when I awoke.

SHE BROUGHT IN THE *Ollie's Daily* and dropped it on the kitchen counter. "Rae, Love," she called, "I've got good news for you!" Raelyn entered from the dining room where her homework was sprawled across the table. Her mother held page five in midair, peck-peck-pecking at the photo. "Ta-da!" she sang. "'Investigators Give Compound A+!'"

Rae gazed at the newsprint. Curly, plump poodles posed on the page, as clean as newly fallen snow, each wearing a bright red ribbon. A picket fence in the foreground was set off by an array of colorful flowers. For a moment, everything went blank. Then a dizzying spiral of shadow and light engulfed the room.

"Rae? Raelyn!" the snap of her mother's fingers appeared before her, and a sharp crease across her brow. "Honey? What just happened?"

Rae was leaning on the counter for support. "It's not true. It's not true, Mom."

"What's not true? What are you talking about?" Her mother's voice was unusually slow and even.

"The photo. The dogs. It's a lie. Or, or. . .a trick, or something."

Ms. Devine placed a hand on her daughter's shoulder and another on her forehead, feeling for clamminess or fever. Rae recoiled. "Honey, I know it's been hard for you these past months. I know you miss her. It's the Unknown, and it makes you think the worst. But it's right here!" She again tapped at the newsprint.

"This is what you—what *we* have waited to hear."

"Stop it!" shouted Raelyn, covering her ears. "I'm telling you, it's not—*real!*" She fled upstairs and slammed her door. How naive to have convinced herself that she could change the course of history.

The news article came up over dinner, but she couldn't tell her parents how, or why, she was so certain about it. She saw the exchanges of concerned, our-daughter-needs-a-shrink glances. Smooth talk could not budge her.

"It's proof they're well cared for. It's clearly a top-notch place," her mother continued to assure her.

"Okay. If this place is so great, then why can't we see it with our own eyes?" Rae demanded.

Her father was rereading the last paragraph. "It says here that it will be open for visitation in the late spring."

"Yeah, and they said way back in January there'd be visiting, too. Remember? There will never be visiting hours. Or a release date. Trust me."

"Honey, listen," her mother said softly, "you can't get this upset about every little thing in life. You'll drive yourself crazy." Then she smiled as if a new, exciting thought had just presented itself. "Have you ever heard about the glass half full? There's a glass of water filled to the halfway mark. One person says, 'The glass is half full.' Another says, "The glass is half empty.' They're both right. But the optimist sees it in a positive way, and the pessimist sees it in a negative way." When her daughter didn't react, she continued, "You see? Please try to be positive."

Her father was studying the dynamic between the two of

them. He shared neither his wife's half-full nor his daughter's half-empty world view. But he was finding it more and more difficult to look his child in the eye. He turned the paper over and sipped his drink.

The following evening at the closed-door legislative session, he and the others sat in their unassigned but regular seats, with Chief Jerkins at the helm. His gestures mimicked Joan's at dinner the day before, only his fingers were fatter, raising page five and tapping heartily at the fluffy pooches. "See there, friends?" His fleshy orange face burst with Glass Half-Fullness. "This ought to put a sock in it!"

Vigil studied his colleagues. Most were following the Leader, but Ms. Cronk's eyes were lowered, and Mr. Morris looked out the window. Vigil shifted several times in his seat before redirecting his focus to Chief Jerkins, who was still pontificating about his successful solution to the Canine Problem.

"Excuse me." All eyes turned to Vigil Devine. The room grew pin-drop still. "When does visitation begin?"

"Visitation?" The members turned to Jerkins.

"Yes."

"*Visitation?*" Jerkins sneered again. His beady blue eyes made their rounds from face to face. Then his lips curled upward, showing the dimple on his left cheek.

Mr. Devine cleared his throat. "As I recall, the Compound was supposed to have visiting hours from the beginning. It's been two and a half months. It's a simple question: What date, precisely, does visitation begin?"

No one had ever before challenged the Chief on the issue. His sharp eyes drilled into Vigil's, and his grin was replaced by a clenched jaw. As much as Vigil wished to turn away, he remained steadfast, unwavering. Mr. Pumpkin Head's jaw relaxed, and his piercing stare broke. He looked calmly around the room, his brow raised in inquiry. "Ladies and Gentlemen of the Legislature," he said in uncharacteristically low tone. "Does this gentleman have the floor?"

Pathetic "No, sirs" fluttered about, lashes downcast.

"I thought not."

A prickle burned across Vigil's forehead where it met his receding hairline. Beads of perspiration formed, dripping between his eyes and down the bridge of his nose. He mopped his face with a napkin. Cautious voices around the room addressed other items on the agenda, but he had lost the thread of the conversation. Within minutes, the meeting was adjourned.

That evening, he typed up his one sentence resignation letter, leaving the date blank. It read:

> Dear Chief Jerkins:
> I hereby resign my position in the Daffy County Legislature effective immediately.
> Very truly yours,
> Vigil W. Devine

He folded it and tucked it in the back reaches of his sock drawer until the time was right.

It didn't take long. A heart-to-heart talk was long overdue with his soon-to-be twelve-year-old. The very next morning, he saw that she had hacked off all of her hair, leaving a dark, uneven mat at the scalp, begging to be noticed. What was happening? All he'd ever had to do was ask. She told him everything. She told him about the failed school club and Mr. E's transfer. She told him about the secret bottom to the food pail and the bangs. She described everything she'd seen inside the Compound and told him about the photographs she'd taken, and her anonymous mailing to the Welfare Society—her last resort for help. The one detail she left out was that she had eaten dog food.

As he listened, Raelyn's stature seemed to grow and his to shrink. She was like Alice, too large to fit into their house in Wonderland, and he, the diminutive toad in the shadow of a mushroom. From what had always been the child's seat at the table, she dwarfed him. All the times she had approached them—seeking answers, begging for guidance, sobbing, arguing--only to be met with his downcast stare. He'd had no idea she had done all those brave things: more evidence of just how asleep he'd been while awake and going through the motions. It had taken a garbage bag of curls to wake him up.

Finally, with a leap of trust, she confided in him about her latest plan—to rescue Penelope from that horrid place. She had the assistance of an unnamed fellow student, she warned, and no one was going to stop them. They could use a reliable grown-up in their corner.

After a long pause, even his voice seemed shadowed and

small. "As an adult, I'd be facing twenty years in prison if I were caught there." He shook his head. "I just can't take that risk. For you or your mother. Or your brother."

"We know. That's why it's going to be us kids."

After another delay, he replied, "I'm concerned about your safety, Raelyn. We're talking about real danger here."

"We know that, too. We're doing it anyway," she announced. "We're saving Penny."

Enter Dad, newest member of the team. "How can I help," he said at last.

Assembled around their dining room table three days later were Raelyn, her father, Gil, and Doc Goodman. Her mother was at work that evening, which was precisely why they were meeting then. They had agreed that she posed a danger to their plan. It wasn't intentional on her part. Like so many others, it happened by osmosis—the hatred of the masses seeping into her mild disdain; the unconscious, gradual assimilation of ideas. In other words, she had become a canine foe.

She wouldn't be home for another two hours.

They had only one opportunity to meet face-to-face to finalize the rescue plan for the following night. There could be no writing, no phone calls, texts, tweets, or emails. All those forms of communication were subject to confiscation. The secret police were onto certain people, and Doc Goodman was one of them. They would be tracking his movements, bugging his phone, intercepting and analyzing his computer activities. So far, the Devines were not on the radar. But just in case Doc had been followed there, a Scrabble board commanded the center of the table. To any outsider, it was harmless fun.

They had a full agenda. As real and dangerous as it was, Raelyn felt as if she were playing a game of Spy or cops and robbers. Her father cleared his throat. "I'll start." He placed three letter tiles on the center of the Scrabble board. They read, C-U-T. "First, the back fence of the Compound must be. . .CUT. . .in advance. That will be the point of ingress and egress."

"What?" Gil asked.

"Entrance and exit."

"C-U-T. That's good, Dad!" Raelyn clapped for a few seconds until she noticed the somber expressions on the others and suddenly felt ridiculous and immature. This wasn't a game, after all. She flicked the phantom hair off her shoulder, forgetting yet again that it wasn't there.

"I'll do that," Doc volunteered. "I can't risk being there for the actual rescue, but I'll cut an opening in the fence."

"Won't they be following you?" Gil asked.

Doc paused. "You're right." He dangled his glasses in his hand. ". . .It's my *car* they follow, really. I'll drive to the supermarket, enter from the front and leave out the back door. I'll have a cab take me close to the Compound, do my business, get back to the store and leave from the front with a grocery bag. I'll wave to the undercover cop waiting for me in the parking lot and go home. How does that sound?"

"Sounds good. Risky, but good." Vigil lifted the Scrabble board slightly and pulled Angie's color-coded map from under it.

He showed it to Doc and pointed to the far boundary opposite the front gate. "You'll want to cut right about. . . here." Doc nodded.

"And," Gil offered, "you'll have to get there, CUT the wire, and get back FAST," he proudly added the F, A and S tiles above the "T" of CUT on the Board:

F

A

S

C U T

Hey, not bad, Gil," Rae exclaimed. "And," she jumped up, picking through the tiles, "make sure it's D, A, R, K—DARK out." She placed the D to the left of the A in FAST and the R and K to the right:

F

D A R K

S

C U T

Her father smiled, then turned serious again. "Then I'll take you two—" he looked at Rae and Gil— "to the Compound in my CAR." He placed the new letters on the board:

F

D A R K

S

C U T

A

R

"And I'll park two blocks away on Spring Street, which is somewhere over here." With his finger, he drew an invisible **X** off the upper right corner of Angie's map. "You two will proceed by foot to the back of the premises and crawl under the cut fence over. . .here."

"Got it," Gil agreed.

"Got it," Rae mimicked. "We'll have to RUN!" The U and the N followed:

F

D A R K

S

C U T

A

R U N

She continued, "and then we get Penelope. . ." but when she looked at the next word she'd created, her head sank into her hands.

"Raelyn?" her father asked softly.

She stared again at the word in front of her. It spelled, D-O-G-S. "It's all wrong. We can't just save Penny and leave everyone else there." She searched the intricacies of the Scrabble board. "We have to find a place for this." The others gazed among each other and felt the heaviness of the room. She was right.

She also was right that D-O-G-S didn't fit anywhere. "Let me help you out," Doc offered. He selected a few letters and placed them on the board under the N in RUN. "The rescue must be completed before dawn, that is, at N, I, G, H, T— NIGHT."

```
          F
      D A R K
          S
        C U T
          A
        R U N
          I
          G
          H
          T
```

He turned to Rae. "Now, your DOGS."

Rae lined her tiles along the G in NIGHT:

```
          F
      D A R K
          S
        C U T
          A
        R U N
          I
      D O G S
          H
          T
```

She continued the story: "Then Gil and I will round up Penny and all of the DOGS—from the barracks and—"

"And," Gil interjected, "get them all to the back D,O,O,R — DOOR—where they'll crawl out to freedom!" He and Rae exchanged high fives.

Vigil's tone turned serious. "It won't be *easy*, kids. You'll be operating under strict time constraints. Saving every one of them is unrealistic."

"But, Dad, we can't leave *anyone* there. They'll die."

"Honey, shh. We'll do our best. But we cannot promise a hundred percent success. Gil needs to get home before anyone misses him. And you both need to show up at school as usual."

Gil was rearranging more letter tiles.

"*Seriously, Dad*? Can't you call in sick for us?"

He shook his head slowly. "I don't think that would be wise."

Doc Goodman agreed. "Remember, the night shift ends at seven o'clock, so the morning guards could arrive as early as 6:30."

"Good point, Ken." Vigil continued, "So you two *must* get back to the car by six o'clock at the very latest." He shifted a stern eye from Rae to Gil. "No exceptions."

"But we *will* rescue them all," Rae insisted on the final word.

As it turned out, it really was the final word of the meeting, because just as she said it (a bit too loudly), the doorknob turned.

All four stared at her mother, Nurse Joan Robin Devine, in hospital scrubs. Gil and Rae's jaws hung open like broken toys. Vigil's hand instinctively slid Angie's map under the Scrabble board.

"Mom! What are *you* doing here?"

"Um, I live here?" She surveyed the scene, suspicious. When was the last time they'd invited the veterinarian and an unfamiliar boy over for a game of Scrabble on a Wednesday night? "What's going on here?" she demanded of her husband.

"We're playing board games," he replied, hoping it would be obvious. "Joan, this is Gil."

"Nice to meet you, Mrs. Devine." His voice was hoarse.

Doc Goodman slid the chair out next to him. "Care to join in?"

"No, no," she said, "really." She was studying the Scrabble Board. "Let's see, what have we here? CUT, DOOR, NIGHT, DARK, DOGS, RUN, FAST, CAR. Interesting." She looked directly at her husband.

He tried to change the subject. "You got off work early. That's terrific."

"It is terrific, isn't it? Fortuitous, even." She smiled ominously at each of them and locked longest on her daughter with the nearly shaven head. Rae swallowed hard. Then her mother turned to Gil. "Gil, is it?" Her eyes shifted to the row of tiles in front of him: "T, H, U, R, S—THURSday. Those can go right. . .here." She moved her finger horizontally from the T along the column that spelled NIGHT. Gil tried to mutter a thank you, but there was no sound.

No one had a response to this wholly unexpected encounter. As complex as the rescue plans were, this confrontation by Ms. Devine was the most challenging moment yet. She spelled T-R-O-U-B-L-E. What had she meant that her arrival home was "fortuitous"? Why the sinister smile? All four of them suffered the same dreaded thoughts: Would she turn them in? She wouldn't *really* have her own husband arrested, would she? Or Doc Goodman, who had risked his life for them only months ago to save Penelope from the fate she now faced?

Then again, Daffy County had gone mad. Neighbors turned on neighbors, friends turned on lifelong friends. And yes, family members not uncommonly turned on their own relatives. Vigil alone knew that, regrettably, his wife had done it once before—to her own son, no less.

Or, they wondered, would she keep their secret, look the other way? Rae recalled her mother sobbing, turning the pages of Penny's photo album that first night amid a carpet of used tissues. There was no telling. One thing they did know was that they couldn't count on her. Vigil made an executive decision. Their rescue mission could not wait until tomorrow night. It had to happen before sunrise.

CHAPTER 17

Plan "B"—A Gutsy, Illegal, But Necessary Adventure

I DREAMED I WAS DYING. *The hospital room was overtaken by beeping machines, and a bright examining light shone down on me. "It won't be long," said a woman who listened through a stethoscope. She wore a long black robe and a flowing headpiece. Someone nearby was praying in a language I didn't recognize.*

Suddenly, the examining light overhead became infinitely brighter. Blinding white rays from the center bulb cast an intense, powerful glow.

"She's gone," the robed woman whispered. At that very instant, I floated upward and my perspective shifted: I was looking down at the bed from suspended whiteness high above the ceiling. I watched, hovering there from that telescoping place as I saw my small body lying on the bed among folded sheets. The woman

kissed my forehead, and her stethoscope became a rosary. I heard a sob from this woman, who had become my mother, and chanting from the corners of the room. Next, I was sucked by tremendous force into the euphoric light. I became one with It.

I understood! But they did not.

I awoke startled in my own bed. I clung to Iggy, rocking myself through an indescribable fear. Had I just died? Was I alive? I pinched myself hard and bore down on the mattress to keep from flying away like a magic carpet. I wept in silence—but as frightened as I was, my tears were of unspeakable joy. It was the strangest, most marvelous moment of my life.

I never told a soul about this dream, except my mother years later. She was reading a book about death after my grandmother died. "Isn't it fascinating?" she exclaimed. "People who've been pronounced dead but are revived all describe a similar experience: They're met by a bright light and a feeling of extreme happiness. Even if they don't believe in God."

"I know. That happened to me once. I saw that light," I told her.

"Don't be silly," she laughed.

HOURS BEFORE DAWN, Rae and her father tiptoed through the dew to the driveway. An upstairs curtain rippled. When they got to Gil's house, his small, dark silhouette appeared from behind a tree. The three drove off, exchanging whispered greetings tainted with dread. They were three human hearts pounding, a percussion of raw nerves.

It was a short ride through the town Rae had known all her life, but nothing looked familiar: Jefferson Elementary School, the library with the *Historic Site* marker in the front, the firehouse and the strip of dollar stores and gas stations. The car was warm, but her teeth chattered. Gil sat beside her in the back seat.

Her father dropped a letter addressed to Chief Ollie Jerkins into the mailbox on the corner of Spring Street. The instant the engine stopped, Rae panicked. Her knees began to spasm uncontrollably, and the knot in her stomach tightened. She had no hair to hide behind. She let out an anguished cry.

She had never felt such fear before. Not on the way up the Rebel Rouser roller-coaster, not at the tipping point looking down at what could only be described as her death, the whole ride only ninety seconds but long enough for an entire life to pass by. Not the moment when Jackson was whisked away behind an iron door, her legs buckling, and those same short cries stifling themselves in her chest. Those had been child's play compared to now. Now, she was staring Terror dead-center in the eye.

She gasped for air, on the cusp of hysteria. Gil remained motionless beside her. Her father pivoted from the driver's seat. "Raelyn. *Rae. Listen to me.*" His command wove its way through internal echoes, each word hanging in isolation: "*You. Don't. Have. To do. This.*"

He was right. She could back out this very instant. She could go home, light and breezy, and dive back under the covers. Yet at the same time, something in his words stirred her. A memory arose from years before. . .an ailing Penelope in her lap, proud faces, encouraging voices off stage: "*You rose to a difficult challenge. . .you could have quit, but you didn't. . .ninety percent of life is showing up.*"

She knew at that moment that she would never retreat. She had a promise to fulfill. This was her mission, her calling. *Penelope was waiting for her.* It had been nearly six months in the works to get her there—a preordained destiny she only vaguely understood: The sign at Blundertown Park, the nasty neighbors. Doc Goodman's midnight visit after the night of broken glass. The collar reducing Penelope to a number, the fake postcard. The buckets and the Mystery Tower, the unexplainable A+ with poodles wearing ribbons. She had tried everything: the Pet Lovers Club, the project in technology class, the risky photographs, the "F" in civics. But she wasn't done yet.

Her terror, she realized, was not about the abstract, unthinkable things that might happen if they got caught. It was about getting caught itself. Someone said there is nothing to fear but fear itself. It had never made sense to her before. The solution was simple: Don't overthink, just do it. *Fear itself! Ninety percent!*

With this new voice, the shaking knees and spasms stopped. *Penelope was calling!*

She and Gil received a final lecture at the driver's window. "Synchronize your cell phones. It's now 3:48 a.m. You have two hours. You *must* be back here by six at the latest. No exceptions. Is that understood?" They nodded. "I'll be waiting. Any delay would be. . . ." His voice trailed off. Then he looked at his daughter. "One hundred percent is not an option. I need your word." She promised. The skin under his eye twitched. "Good luck, you two." As she was about to leave, he reached out, grabbed her hand, and squeezed it with all his might.

"*Ow,* Dad."

She and Gil hiked a few steps in the dark before breaking into a sprint. Gil was instantly ahead of her. "Hey!" she called in a throaty whisper. He reached back and grabbed her hand, propelling her forward into, for her, a very swift pace. They only stopped when they reached the far corner of the Compound. They searched the back fence with their flashlights until they located the cut in the wire, courtesy of Doc Goodman. They manipulated the wire, bending it up and to the side. Then they got down on all fours and crawled in.

What had not been discussed at the meeting (thanks to the untimely interruption by her mother) were the critical details of detaining the Night Guard before rescuing the dogs. But Rae and Gil formulated a vague plan. It was fraught with disastrous possibilities, but it was the only one they could think of. They made their way silently, clearing a diagonal through the spacious field. She kept right up with him, their phones bobbing unsteady light in front of them beneath a canopy of stars.

"Watch out!" Rae called. He saw it, too, inches in front of his sneaker: a wide, open pit smack in the middle of the meadow, camouflaged by darkness. Its depth was unknown.

"Whoa." He stopped right at the edge. "Where did *that* come from?" They guided each other around it and continued more cautiously through the field and between the buildings. They reached the Security Station where they hoped the Night Guard would be sleeping, as Officer Budd had said. The only light on the grounds came from the office window on the second floor. She inched the front door open and listened. It was the joyous sound of snoring! She flashed Gil an "A-Okay."

They removed their shoes and tiptoed up the stairs. The snores came from *Her Room* to the right, where she had been held under lock and key as Angie Quinn. The door was wide open. The light from the hallway revealed an intimidating mound on the front cot, the bearded face snoring directly at them.

In the office, the guard's cell phone sat on the desk, and the key hung in place on the wall hook. She grabbed it, shuffled back to Gil, and gave him a nod. He closed the door without a sound. She turned the key full circle until it clicked. They hurried downstairs and into the chilly darkness. The Night Guard was locked in.

She took a breath. "Whew. That was easy."

"Yeah, but it could have been—"

"But it wasn't."

"I know. But he *could've* been—"

"But he wasn't."

"I'm just saying—" Gil waited for an interruption— "that we're lucky, that's all." It was only a matter of time before the guard would awake and realize his predicament.

Only then did they acknowledge the smell. It was the same stench that had overcome her the last time she was there. They'd been so consumed by their fear and risky business that the traces of decay and burning had gone unnoticed.

Gil gagged and covered his face. "Ugh! What *is* that?"

"Not now. Let's focus, okay?" she said, blocking her nose as well.

The next phase of the Rescue was, of course, the rescue. Neither of them was prepared for the emotional impact Phase II would have. She'd been there before, but for Gil, it was like he'd stepped into a foreign land, eerie and deserted. He stayed unusually, even rudely, close to her, his arm rubbing her shoulder. In the real world it would've been a boundary violation, "getting into her space." But neither of them even noticed.

"What do we do now?" he asked, as if they'd just landed on Mars by complete accident.

She surveyed the grounds, at a loss herself where to begin. All the details they'd gone over had completely vanished. The beam of her flashlight traveled slowly, left to right, highlighting the structures opposite them: The *Groom Room,* the *Storage Shed, Barracks I (Barracks II* was out of view), and further back, the *Mystery Tower* looming high above. She switched off the light. Neither spoke. The gray buildings blended beautifully with the dark, charcoal sky like two-dimensional cookie-cutter outlines, a child's simple drawing. It looked like the map she would have drawn. Or a respectable artist's work, *Study of Silhouettes, Pre-Dawn, Charcoal on paper.* None of it seemed real. Her brain was strangely vacant.

She searched overhead, perhaps for a hint of divine guidance from the heavens. But all she found there was a giant question mark, the tilt of the Big Dipper: *You Are on Your Own.*

"Um. . .okay," she directed, "you take Barracks I. I'll take Barracks II. We go in and—" she paused— "and we don't think, got it? And we get the dogs out. And we find Penelope."

"Do you think they're—"

"Gil!" she shouted. "I just said, 'We don't think,' and then you say something about thinking. We just go in and do it. Like robots." She glanced at her phone. "We're wasting time." She attacked him with a commanding bear hug, fists clenched around his shoulders and heels off the ground. A warm comfort engulfed her but vanished in an instant. She ran off past Barracks I to the building behind it. She stopped at the door of Barracks II and held her breath.

The door creaked as it opened. She scanned the interior with her flashlight. The shaft of light met one sight, then another, then another: Dogs. Dogs everywhere. Emaciated, lying on top of one another, large black orbs staring at her, bewildered and nearly lifeless on the bare floor. Everywhere she looked, they were there. There must have been well over a hundred of them.

"Penny?" She heard a thin, quivering voice. Whose voice was this, what was this hellish place? "Penny, come," the voice called again, this time louder. A general stirring began, some shifting here, some rustling there. As her night eyes began to adjust, the floor became a sea of fluttering movement. She heard her own heart pounding. "Come, guys," she urged. "*Come!*"

Then they came. First just a handful, limping, dragging themselves across to her, stepping over each other. She heard an awakening of light breathing, low moaning. Someone sneezed in the far corner. Someone whimpered. Next thing she knew, she was surrounded by dozens of four-leggeds. "Come!" She recognized a measure of hope in the voice as the entire floor seemed to swell up at once. It was a mass movement of weakness that rolled toward her, like a salty tide seeping into the sand beneath her feet, caressing her toes, hugging her thighs. Salt trickled down her face. She was on her knees, her arms and lanky elbows extended everywhere, caressing the uncaressable skin and bone.

She was the Pied Piper. She beckoned and coaxed them out the door, and they followed her. Behind Barracks I, behind the *Spa* and the *Mystery Tower* and to Doc Goodman's secret door, lay their pathway to freedom. The small herd tried to keep pace. A few tails even fluttered, and the wails and barks grew stronger.

When they reached the opening in the fence, they stopped. Some lay down, already exhausted.

"Go," Rae commanded. "Go on. *Now!*" Confused faces studied her. *"Fetch!"* She pantomimed tossing a stick high into the darkness beyond the fence. *"Fetch!"* She made more throwing motions. "Go *get* it!" A wave of panic crept through her; every second was critical. *"What's the matter with you?"* she cried. She began steering them through the fence, one by one, careful to avoid their protruding hip bones. So far, none of them was Penelope. They reached the other side in painfully slow procession, but it was working.

When she finished the line, she turned back to gather more.

Dogs were wandering aimlessly all over the place, stumbling, wailing, whimpering. She worked tirelessly. Back and forth, she relayed from the dorm, rounding them up and pushing them out. Some began to follow each other out the door, but this was going to be a race against time—and she had noted that some of the freed dogs were merely lingering on the other side instead of galloping off into the forest and toward their second chance of life. That would be the last phase of their mission, if they ever made it that far.

Barracks II was finally empty. The black sky had become a deep violet gray. She had not seen Gil. She had not seen Penelope. And dawn was only a gradual curve of Earth away.

As she ran to check on Gil, a voice boomed and cursed from high. It was the night guard, his hairy face large in the shattered window, his fist violently pounding the air. His torso looked about to leap out of the window frame when he spotted her. He shouted, among obscenities, "This is an order! Cease and desist! You'll pay for this," his arms flailing about from his helpless post.

She darted into Barracks I. It was still completely full. Gil sat among the victims, his head hanging in his lap. "Gil!" she shouted. He didn't move. "What the hell are you doing?" He raised his head, but his eyes were shut. He looked almost as pitiful as the company he was supposed to be saving. She slapped him forcefully and yanked him until he rose, obligingly, to his feet. "I *told* you! Just *do* it."

Strands of hair hung over his brow, fluttering like the wings of a wounded bird. She realized he was crying. He was nearly inaudible, "They don't—don't even *look* like dogs. . .I can't—"

"You can! And you will. Now!" What was she going to do, are you kidding me? It was impossible to do it alone. This entire mission would be a failure. Penelope's image blurred before her. It wanted to float away, but she kept pulling it back to her: *Don't go. Please don't go, Penny. Don't give up on me.* Gil was an oversized rag doll, his broad arms hanging uselessly at his sides and his hair aflutter. As she stared at the pathetic figure, something large and ugly rose to her chest. From a deep, shameful place she didn't know existed, cruel desperation took over. "Pee Pants," she cried. "You're nothing but a stupid Pee Pants!" She was staring him down. Suddenly she was unstoppable. Yes, she *would* go there. She mocked and taunted in a snotty, sing-songy chant that every child instinctively knows: "Pee Pants, Pee Pants, Nothing but a Pee-Pants!" She threw a quick jab into his chest. He didn't even defend himself! Her taunts grew louder: "Nothing but a Pee-Pants." her arms swinging wildly, slapping and jabbing his unprotected body. Next, she was circling him, hopping on one foot, then the other, as she twirled, diving in for a slap here, a punch there, belting out the schoolyard tune at the top of her lungs.

It worked.

"*Stop it, damn it!*" he screeched. "I am *not* a Pee Pants!" His fist was mid-air, ready to strike.

The room went silent. They stood face to face, surrounded by a very captivated audience. Something like a giggle caught deep in her chest. Then in Gil's. "Wow." He struck his forehead with the palm of his hand. *"Twilight Zone."* He gazed at the mass of forms surrounding them. Then he looked away. "You're a real *you-know-what,* you know." He swung his hair skillfully around so it flipped off his forehead. He was back to the Gil she needed.

In the so-called real world, an embrace like that between two sixth-graders at Blundertown Middle School might have generated some online drama. But there, in the privacy of that filthy prison, time stopped for them.

Or so they would have wished. It was 5:03.

While the world slept, the two of them worked quickly in Barracks I just as she had in Barracks II, corralling masses of innocent prisoners through the back fence. She looked each one directly in the face. With each face, her heart grew a little heavier and more frantic. None of these was Penelope, either. When the dorm had largely thinned out, Gil took command. He offered to finish up while Rae tended to the stragglers outside who had fallen from the pack. They were walking in circles or lying down, scattered throughout the grounds.

When finished, he closed up Barracks I and joined her. He knew exactly what she meant when she looked at him. "No Penelope. Not yet," he told her.

"Are you sure?"

"Yeah."

"One hundred percent positive? Did you look at every single one?"

"Yeah. I did."

"What if you didn't recognize her?" She looked ready to cry.

"Hey." He put his arm on her upper back, where a thick cloak of curls used to be. "I know her. I wouldn't miss her. We just haven't found her yet, that's all." But his words offered only a sliver of comfort. He suggested, "She's probably already out. Maybe she slipped past us." There it was, the paltry Glass Half Full. His phone said 5:37. "Let's run through the smaller buildings and then get out of here."

"What? *No!*" Rae snapped. "We can't leave all these wanderers. There's still, I don't know, thirty, forty? We can't just leave them."

"Most of them can barely walk. Remember what your dad said."

"We have to try. One of them is Penelope."

"Okay," he hesitated, "but we only have, like, twenty minutes. We've gotta hustle."

It was a relay without anyone to pass to. He carried a dog in each arm, and she carried another and a flashlight. At that rate, they had to make over a dozen trips to clear the place out. They sprinted. Even for Gil it was arduous. For Rae, it was sheer adrenaline. They dashed back and forth, scooping up dogs and racing to the exit, back and forth, pick up, drop, repeat, an egg toss at gunpoint. The animals had to be treated just as delicately, too, and each one was ruled out as Penelope. Each time they reached the fence, the barks and wails grew louder. Soon, someone would be calling the police. They were clammy with sweat.

Suddenly, Gil came to an abrupt stop. "It's time." She

bumped into him, full force, from behind. "Watch where you're going!" he accused.

"*Me?*" she shouted. He was so unbelievable.

THE YARD WAS EMPTY. They'd rescued them all. Rae fell to the ground, utterly defeated. "Where is she?" she began to sob. An expanse of clouds had risen from behind a steep hill, creating a vibrant backdrop of crimson. It cast a strange other-worldliness over the vacant field.

Gil stood over her. "Uh, we really have to go," he urged. She continued sobbing. "C'mon. It'll be alright. But you have to stand up." He waited helplessly. "Don't cry."

"Why not? You did!" She wept.

He tried to think of something he could use against her from kindergarten, but nothing came to him. Then something much more recent popped up. "Hey. I could call you a 'Dog Food Eater,' you know." She stopped to listen. "And start singing like a lunatic." She sniffled. "Want me to?"

"No."

"And hop around you like an Energizer bunny, and throw some punches. Want me to?"

"No."

"Okay, then. On the count of three, get up. Or I will." He began, "One," and paused. "Two." She didn't move. "Two and a half." Still nothing. He sighed, "Damnit, Raelyn. Two and three-quarters."

She lifted a wimpy arm to him.

He grabbed it and pulled her up. "Three." He wiped away her tears with his thumbs.

They had six minutes left. They would make a quick round through the outbuildings on the chance they would find her. It would be their final effort.

Each building contained shocking revelations. The Groom Room was full of fur. Literally. Rae recalled how the groomer had shaved all the dogs—a solution to flea infestation, it was claimed. It was this cruel act that had triggered her own statement of solidarity with scissors to her own scalp. The fur was stuffed into clear garbage bags stacked from floor to ceiling and labeled, *For Shipment: Ollie's Upholstery, Inc.* A large pile of loose fur had been swept to one corner of the room.

"What in the—" Gil was staring intently at the swept pile.

"They shave them because—" He blocked her with his arm, still eyeing the corner of the room. She saw it too—a slight movement. Gil walked toward it with his flashlight. The pile stirred a little more, and out popped a skinny, jet-black puppy. He was furless and trembling. Two tiny, black circles stared up at Gil.

"Hi, little guy," Gil cooed and squatted in front of him. The puppy emitted a faint, high-pitched whimper. "You're clever, aren't you? You found the warmest place in this hellhole, under all this fluffy fur." He scooped him into his arms.

"OMG," Rae came closer. "He's probably only a few months old."

He tucked him into his jacket. "I'm taking him out of here. How about you check the next building real quick, and I'll check those other two on the way out." She conceded. "And then, Rae, we've gotta get to the car. We have less than four minutes. Meet you there?"

"Got it."

The Storage Shed was organized into piles. Her flashlight revealed a large mound of unused toys: balls of all colors and sizes, braided ropes, rubber bones, and rawhides. Another pile contained wrapped presents, most of them in holiday paper received but never opened, and countless unopened letters addressed to "Taddie," "Archibald," "Gertie." The lump in her throat made it painful to swallow. Surely, buried among these things were her letters and gifts to Penelope. A third pile contained leashes, brushes, nail clippers, and toothbrushes. The largest was a mountain of clothes and bedding.

"Hello? Penelope?" she called, hoping that Penny was another smart one hiding in a warm place. She rummaged on all fours through the pile of clothes. "Penelope, it's me." She crawled deeper into it, calling out again and again. No one was there. She dug herself out, sobbing, and closed the door behind her.

Once out on the dirt road, she realized she was missing her cell phone. She must have lost it somewhere in the heap. She returned to search for it, on all fours again, burrowing herself in the dense mounds of fabrics. Had she left the flashlight on or turned it off? she wondered. She saw no glow anywhere. For some reason, she started to panic. She began flinging items every which way, still buried among the garments. It had to be in here somewhere. The more she dug herself in, the more determined she was to find it.

It was getting warmer and stuffier, and she was heaving for air. It occurred to her that she could suffocate in here. What a horrible, senseless way to die. Suddenly, her phone sounded. She followed the muffled ring until she located it, then breast-stroked her way out of the heap and raced out of the building.

She was drenched in sweat, relieved to be in open air. It was 6:02. The lit screen from Gil screamed, *WHERE R U??* Her father would be furious. She'd become so sidetracked; what had she been thinking? She didn't need her phone. She didn't even need the flashlight anymore. The sky had lightened several shades to deep periwinkle. Dawn was moments away. The night guard was hunched over in the upstairs window. When he saw her, he began muttering anew a string of garbled obscenities, but his voice was weak, his resolve depleted. ". . .Won't get away with this. . . ." was all she could make out.

As she ran past Barracks I, she stopped. Her eyes fixed on the closed door. She glanced in the direction of the fence, where Gil was long gone. High on the horizon, the world continued awakening before her very eyes. That was the thing about sunrise: You could watch patiently for a whole hour and nothing much happened; then in a matter of seconds, it was over. If only she had just a few more of those precious moments. Several remaining stars twinkled and lingered in the dawn, trying to hold on.

Her phone said 6:05.

She entered Barracks I.

The open door offered some light to the center of the room, but left large interior wedges still in darkness. Gil had assured her that he'd given this building a final check. The dorm appeared bare except for a few worn rags flung carelessly about—remnants of what the occupants might have tried to pass for blankets or comfort in another lifetime. Yet the walls seemed to pulsate and breathe. In the darkness, the hollows moaned to escape their own shadows. Ghosts now occupied this place and always would.

She stood there longer than time permitted. Gil would have chased as many dogs as possible into the woods before meeting her father. Any dog who meandered near the fence probably would be shot once the police were alerted to the break-in. No one would be returning for her. She remained there in a trance.

Something drew her attention to the far corner. She would never know what caused her to turn there, for it was neither sound nor scent, and as dark as charcoal. She moved steadily toward it. On the floor was a clump, a small mound. She tried to adjust her sight in the darkness, but all she could make out was that it appeared motionless. She knelt down to study it more closely. It was a series of curved sticks, lined up one against the other, forming an encasement of sorts. With the tips of two fingers, she felt a thin, velvety covering over the curves. She identified them instantly as ribs. Her eyes, still struggling to see, followed along the dark mass lying there. She was now touching a jawline that protruded like the dull side of a knife. Above the jaw was Penelope's left eye. It was open.

Rae pressed her own face to the thin facial structure below, held her breath and listened. She smelled a warm, shallow exhale. Penelope was alive! She scooped the weightless body into her arms and caressed her in her lap. She began rocking gently.

How long she held Penny there, rocking and humming in private reunion, she wouldn't know. But suddenly it ended. As if a hypnotist snapped her fingers, she stood up, protecting Penelope close to her chest. She whisked a ragged bedsheet from the floor, wrapped it around Penny, and slipped out into the pastel morning.

She wandered in delirium toward the back fence, where the hundreds of other dogs had already escaped. Their whimpers and calls echoed from the forest beyond. Sirens wailed in the distance. Initially the sounds came from behind her. Then they came from in front of her, where she was heading, instantly drowning out the animals' cries. She began to run. The police sirens bellowed now in full, surround sound, increasing in terror as they grew.

She scurried through the back fence on her knees, with Penny huddled to her chest. Several confused dogs met them at the opening. Something crunched under her kneecap.

"Raelyn!" It was her father shouting amidst the clamor. His blurry figure appeared at the corner, and she realized her glasses were gone. His wide, sweeping arms beckoned. A series of loud "pops" echoed in the air, reverberating deep into the channels of her ears. He rushed toward her in slow motion, his arm commanding a halt at the flashing vehicles, his mouth shouting something. But she heard nothing.

She was bouncing in his broad embrace, the torn bedsheet draped around her shoulders. A tremendous roar consumed the world. Suddenly, an intense, bright light appeared from above. It hovered over them, suspended and radiating. Her father ran directly toward it, the wind blasting with centrifugal force. She was lifted high above his head, the torn, white sheet whipping around her like an angel's wings taking flight. Another set of arms grabbed her from the blinding light source above. She found herself in the arms of medical personnel dressed in white. It was her mother.

"Go!" Nurse Devine shouted to the pilot. The helicopter lifted away from the chaotic world below.

Rae was seated in back with Penelope swaddled in her lap, and the aircraft shook and vibrated. Through the deep rumbling of the engine, the pilot's cries trickled through: "We need," his thin voice bellowed— "Good God, what a sight. The dogs. . . send medical supplies, water. . . ." She noticed the sharp smell of disinfectant and her right leg propped in her mother's lap. Nurse Devine was wiping her calf with a soaked red cloth. It occurred to her that she had no feeling in any places her mother touched.

"A bullet must have ricocheted off something," her mother reported in skilled calm. "You'll be fine, baby." But tears pooled at her lower eyelids, ready to topple over the edges. She began wrapping gauze around the wound.

"Mom. Penny needs water." Her voice made no sound amidst the blaring of the engine. A paper cup appeared. Penelope immediately began lapping it up with sloppy licks, sending water flying everywhere. A dark, cold spot appeared in the crook of Rae's pants. She pictured Gil on the kindergarten bus. Then she pictured him in their agonizing moments in Barracks I, their laughter so wildly out of place. Both seemed equally a lifetime ago. She began to giggle. Her mother examined her face with a clinician's eye and a worried frown.

Rae turned away and looked out the small, curved window. They were flush along the tree line near the peak of a hill. The sky was awash in shades of pink, diffusing downward in wide bands. But as the helicopter cleared the jagged tops of the trees, she blinked at the breathtaking sight on the other side: The entire sky was transformed into an expansive burst of light —an immense arc of fiery orange and yellow emanating infinite power in all directions. It was the Earth's awesome halo, the morning sun.

"Wow." She was transfixed.

"Don't look directly at it, sweetie," her mother cautioned. "It can blind you."

Rae turned to her. The awakening universe cast iridescence in her mother's eyes, a watery, gilded green. She studied the colors, the gradations of lightness and depths of the first set of eyes she had ever looked into nearly twelve years before. Amazing, all this time, and her mother wasn't a bird, after all. Rae was gazing into the face of a swan, a majestic Trumpeter queen. Holding Penelope, she scooted toward her and leaned into the pillow of downy feathers, the wide expanse of wing white as snow. Her head was suddenly very heavy. It settled into the warm whiteness, and her eyelids drifted closed.

"Hello, there, My Lady," she heard the Swan Mother say. "Welcome home. . . ." But the voice grew faint, falling out of range. It was the last thing she remembered.

CHAPTER 18

Penelope Park

A CYNIC WOULD SAY IT WAS THE PAIN MEDICATION. *But in the hospital that night, something wonderful happened. My Glitter came back!*

First, it was just a few blindingly bright specks. What is this? My curiosity was awakened. Then, like before, out popped a small group here and another group there of vibrant, multi-colored sparkles, spinning and dancing. They poured out in abundance and grew into an amazing kaleidoscopic masterpiece: fiery turquoise, scarlet, emerald, bronze and copper, lavender, magenta, silver, azure, chartreuse, and gold. The colors shone through as if beaming from an intense, infinite light source, every particle glowing and twinkling a thousand-fold. It was a breathtaking sight to behold.

The amazing thing is that the Glitter came back to me as if it had never left. It occurred to me then, as I watched in the pitch darkness, that perhaps it had never disappeared after all. Perhaps it had always been there, off to the side, in the depths of my despairing mind. I just hadn't looked hard enough for it. When I became disheartened with the world, I'd forgotten to look, and eventually forgot it even existed.

But there it was: right in front of me, my welcome home celebration!

I fell into a comforting sleep and began a whole new series of dreams. Many of them have been remarkable, fantastic. And many have come true.

Raelyn left the hospital on crutches with get-well balloons, cards, and bundles of bouquets from friends and strangers alike. She also left with a shiny, silver bullet the size of a baby pea—the one that had lodged itself in the back of her right calf, a souvenir for her scrapbook. She would have a life-long scar there, like Mr. Pumpkin Head, eight stitches apiece.

Penelope came home a couple of weeks later, after being nursed back to health by Doc Goodman. Doc had immediately opened an emergency clinic and treated all of the survivors, many of whom, like Penny, had been airlifted or otherwise transported from the Compound to safety. Once they were stabilized, Doc kept the clinic open indefinitely as a welcome center. For those convalescing, there were warm bubble baths and a beautiful, hand-stitched scarf for each and every one. Two scrumptious meals a day! Daily walks and games of catch. New beds, brushings as their tufts of fur grew back. And as soon as Penelope was well enough, she and Raelyn taught them all how to spell.

Swarms of volunteers came to help. Gil was among them, as was Night, the little black puppy he'd rescued from the pile of fur and instantly adopted. Night pranced a half-step behind him everywhere he went. Her parents were there, of course. Even the neighbor, Kelly Davis, dared to show up once (gag), always aligning herself with whatever team was winning. Megan, Cierra, and Angelica were among the volunteers, too. Angie couldn't help with the baths because she'd come directly from the nail salon. But she was there nonetheless, side-by-side with her best friend.

"Here to give moral support?" Raelyn teased. Her stylish new crop highlighted her cheekbones and radiant smile.

And one afternoon, in walked Jackson Devine, the prodigal son. He lifted Penelope gently to his chest. When he attempted to do the same with his sister, Raelyn squirmed out of his embrace and punched him in the arm. "Hey, Jackass. Better late than never."

She wanted her prize. She had more than earned it. She unfolded a piece of paper from Doc's desk with the answers to his treasure hunt. "G," "E," "I," "V," and the fifth was a question mark: "?". She had solved that one in a dream a few days after the rescue:

> *Look overhead in Springtime*
> *For the Great Bear in the sky*
> *A tilt of your head*
> *(You should be in bed)*
> *Marks who-what-when-where-why.*

Jackson's "Great Bear," of course, was Ursa Major, the most easily identified constellation—also known as the Big Dipper. At a certain angle, it became the abstract question mark of the heavens, the existential symbol humans have faced throughout history. It was that very same question mark that she'd seen during the rescue mission that desperate April night. At the time, she'd thought it was a useless, even cruel, response to her plea for help. But perhaps she had misunderstood. Perhaps it had been heaven's eternal question back to her: *How can I help you?*

"So," Raelyn guessed, "I think they probably spell, 'G, I, V, E, ?' But I don't know what it means."

"That's because you're missing the answer to my last clue," her brother explained. "How come?"

"Tell me you're kidding, Jackass?" She pulled an envelope from the drawer. "I never even looked at the last clue. I've been a little busy, you know." She tore it open and read his hand-written words aloud:

> *I wear my feelings on my arm*
> *Both my sadness and my charm*
> *But something guides me there, as well*
> *The right direction it does tell.*
> *N, S, E, West*
> *These points know what's best.*

As she read, Jack flexed his left biceps to show off his tattoo. She broke into a smile. "Oh! I get it. It's the 'cardinal' points."

But the pause on his face told her she was wrong, and a "C" wouldn't fit anywhere. North, South, East, West, she thought. And then she knew the answer. "Four. These 4 points!" She continued, "so the final answer is: 'GIVE 4?' Or, '4-GIVE?' Like, 'do you FORGIVE?'" She bounced off her heels in triumph. "I'm right! Am I right?"

He still remained silent.

Suddenly, a flash of rage overtook her. "*No.* I will never forgive. *Any of them!*"

Again, he said nothing, but his eyes were misty.

". . .Jack?"

He held out his arms to her.

"Do I forgive. . .*you*?" She gathered all ten of his fingers and squeezed. "*You*, yes." They shared several moments of silence, knuckles knotted. Then she tossed all hands up to the wind and announced, "Enough of that. How about my treasure!"

Jackson pulled something out of his back pocket. Initially, it reminded her of one of his magic tricks, where an endless string of fabrics came slithering out of his jacket sleeve. But this wasn't magic. He gave it to her. It was a long silken scarf, an exquisite rainbow of stunning beauty. It seemed to breathe in her hands. She examined the tiny, imperfect stitching and brought it to her face. It was as soft as Penelope's ears.

THE BLUNDERTOWN COMPOUND was shut down for good. All of them were. Yes, there had been others scattered across the entire state—pin marks on an expanding map in Chief Jerkins' private office. Once Penelope's compound fell, the others followed like dominoes. The locals learned that, while resistance and rescue efforts had been made at many of the compounds, the Blundertown Compound rescue had by far been the most successful.

At first, people went out of their way to avoid the streets on which the wretched ghost towns stood. Over time, though, they went out of their way to travel down those very roads, to peek through the padlocked fences, to bear witness, in a small way, to a most shameful time in their history.

Ollie Jerkins went to trial, as did Angie's father, Ted Quinn. They now live somewhere upstate with a huge, smelly cafeteria and a Wall of Vending Machines. They arrived there at about the time Jackson celebrated his seventeenth birthday at home, just as he had predicted. Angelica will see her father age over the course of her bi-weekly visits, but he'll be released one day. He expressed genuine remorse and has come to see that dogs were our earliest best friends and are no less worthy than himself.

Mr. Pumpkin Head, on the other hand, will grow very, very old there. He has become famous—or rather, infamous; far and wide, his murderous ways have come to be known as Ollie's Folly, and he the Most Despicable Man Alive. With not the slightest interest in changing his heart, he will never be released in this lifetime.

The Canine Laws were abolished, and the parks once again welcomed dogs of every kind. Blundertown Park was renamed *Penelope Park*. She, Atlas, Prince, and Night meet there almost daily. As a member of The Underground Squad who lived to tell her tale, she enjoys a certain cachet and occasionally draws a small crowd. *We almost made it,* she tells them. *Our tunnel was nearly complete!* But more often than not she lies under a shade tree and studies the smell of worms under the grass, the beetles, the sweet roots sprawling beneath the surface. She watches the younger ones play and frolic. The truth is, she will never be quite the same. Her plight aged her immensely. None of them are the same, really; how could they be? For, right behind their excitable tails and animated eyes is a whiff of sadness that will forever belong to them—a sadness they have for keeps.

But, oh, the puppies! Over time, there are more and more puppies at Penelope Park. And many more at all the newly opened parks throughout the land. They trip and stumble over their oversized paws and banter in high-pitched yelps. These pups are once removed from their parents' ordeal, and their litters will be twice removed from their grandparents'. But make no mistake: That ordeal remains an integral part of them, and is never far away. As they play, chase, dig, sniff, guard, and bark as puppies always have, the stories and histories are passed down from one generation to the next. This, to ensure: *Never again!*

And guess what? Penelope was finally allowed to sleep upstairs in Raelyn's bedroom. Her luxurious bed, fit for a queen, remained permanently at Rae's bedside. Really, Mom, Dad? It took all of *this* for you to finally say yes?

EPILOGUE

SO, YOU SEE, ALL OF MY CHILDHOOD *dreams came true— the good, the bad and the ugly: from plunging into the deepest pit to viewing my life through the eyes of God.*

I ask myself, did saving Penelope and her companions, when so many others were killed, tip the scales of justice at all? How many good deeds are needed to overcome the weight of evil? To restore equilibrium?

There is a granite plaque where the Blundertown Compound once stood. It memorializes the victims and recognizes the individuals (one being me) who saved the last of them on that early morning Aprils ago.

But when I look in the mirror each day, I don't see a hero. I see two of me: one, losing my balance and falling full speed into a black hole; the other, climbing out—first one muscled grip, then a foot, another grip, and so forth, upward.

After all, it was Angelica's dad—a most loving, doting father and husband, the one who brought a dozen roses to every per-

formance, who sculpted a palace out of mud with his bare hands, who attended church every Sunday, the very same man who ultimately came to account.

In the mirror, I see my family staring blankly in my direction in their winter coats on a snow-covered walk, with me beckoning from the tulips and the bursting, spring magnolia. The Devine SUV, me in the driver's seat(!) on our way to a dangerous mission. I see my parents, bobble heads both, yessing their bosses and worrying about their children. My father keenly watching the ups and downs and inching one direction over the other. My lovely, steadfast, but stubborn mother, who came through only in the very end, but with guns blazing: what style! I see my brother, who forfeited the strings of his own life for a time but quickly found his way, a king among misfits spinning straw into gold from behind bars. No matter the constraints, there is always something you can do.

Next in my view appears Angie, who drew her own safe line in the sand. And Gil, a cocky middle-school athlete with a heart of gold, who wept like a baby. In the looking glass, I see Kelly Davis, once Penelope's favorite neighbor. Masked, she was phony and warm; unmasked, true and cold. I see the inhabitants behind the curtained windows along the edge of Blundertown where the Compound used to be, eyes, ears and noses pinched shut.

Penelope is before me now, the face of dignified simplicity, my true best friend. She would have dug to the ends of the Earth for me had it been the other way around.

Finally, my twenty-year-old face takes on the features of Mr.

Pumpkin Head himself, whose sick obsessions got the best of him and whose charisma and hatred got the best of everyone else. And selfless Doc Goodman, who saw things as they were, and are, and never wavered.

In other words, when I look in the mirror, I see you and me.

When you close your eyes at night before drifting off to sleep, can you see the Glitter?

About the Author

Born and raised in Michigan, Jane M. Bloom has spent most of her adult life in the beautiful Catskills of upstate New York, enjoying the balance of life, work, and family. As a practicing attorney, she has represented hundreds of children (as well as adults) in Sullivan County, where she resides with her husband, daughter, and two dogs. She earned her bachelor's degree from the University of Michigan and her law degree from Pace University School of Law.

Ms. Bloom is equally passionate about the big things—Alaska's mighty glaciers; attending the largest march in U.S. history—as she is the small things like walking the dogs or hiking to the waterfall near her home. She enjoys music festivals, travel, and volunteering for Guiding Eyes for the Blind.

Visit her website at *janembloom.com.*

CPSIA information can be obtained
at www.ICGtesting.com
Printed in the USA
JSHW021222130220
4200JS00003B/4